THE EDEE STORY

CLARE MERRETT

Paperback ISBN: 978-1-9163021-2-9
eBook ISBN: 978-1-9163021-3-6

Editor: Kate Angelella
Cover design and illustration: Anna Woodbine
Proofreading: Kate Habberley
Print edition formatting: Stephanie Drake

For my family

1

"Here," said the optician, opening a clear plastic wallet and pulling the glasses from it with more arm movements than such a task surely required. "Are you excited?"

"Er," said Edee.

The optician pulled the arms open, looked all over the glasses, and held them just in front of her face. "Every time, I think what a feat of engineering. What an invention of mankind. Sorry! Humankind. What perfection."

He was making it sound like Edee was about to adorn her face with a piece of artwork or something. Not that she had to wear these *things* because her eyes didn't work properly. Well, actually, she was perfectly happy with how they worked thanks all the same. Sure, some stuff was a bit blurry. But it had always been blurry—fifteen years of blurry—and, until a couple of weeks ago, it had never occurred to her that it mattered. Blurriness was soft round the edges. Fuzzy. Nice.

It turned out, however, that whatever blurry was, it wasn't enough. Everyone had to see things in full, super-duper, crystal clarity. Because . . . everyone else said so. And now she had to walk about with a sign on her face telling the world that she naturally saw in a blur.

"Such a good choice," continued the optician, twisting the glasses one way and then the other. "You've obviously got an eye for this sort of thing." He chuckled.

"Come on," said her mum. "How about you just put them on."

Edee glanced at her with a look that tried to say I-would-if-I-could-get-them-away-from-this-job-loving-weirdo. Mum raised an eyebrow. The optician was still gazing at the frames. If Lucie were here, she would have snapped her fingers in front of his face.

Lucie was not here. She was five hundred miles away. It might as well be a million. It felt like a million.

Edee's throat tightened and her eyes tingled. Not again. She couldn't cry in an optician's. She *couldn't*. The man was going to be staring at her face any second; never mind that Mum was hovering at her shoulder. She pushed her tongue against her teeth to quell the tingling (it had saved her a ton of times in the last two weeks), then pulled the frames from his hands and shoved them onto her nose. The sooner this happened, the sooner they could get out of here.

She blinked.

"Oh, yes," said the optician. "They most certainly suit you. What do you think, Mum?"

Edee blinked again. The tightness and tingling had, for the moment at least, disappeared. Surprise was apparently more effective than the teeth trick.

"Oh, look," said the optician. "She's lost for words. It's quite overcoming isn't it, being able to see this clearly. Life changing! Take a look out there, through the door. See how clear the big wide world is."

Edee did not look outside. She looked at the optician.

Because, because . . . he was now sitting behind, no, *inside* . . . something.

A something that went from his head to his feet.

A something that was see-through but unmistakably there.

The whatever-it-was followed the line of his body, jutting around the angles of his elbows, knees, and shoulders. The chair was not included, just him. She raised a hand and moved it forward. Instead of stopping at the . . . film? . . . wall? . . . her fingers connected with his arm.

"Edee!" said Mum. "What are you doing? I'm so sorry. Edee!"

"Sorry," muttered Edee.

"Oh, no problem. Depth perception can seem a little different at first," said the optician, discreetly rubbing his arm.

His arm inside the something.

What on earth? Who was this weirdo, this new level of weirdo-ness?

"Now, how do they fit?"

She recoiled a tiny amount as he bent forward and tugged on the arms. The frame slightly slid over her ears. At the same time, she gingerly scuffed a foot forward. The toe of her shoe pushed on the whatever-it-was and against his laces. He didn't seem to notice.

"Not too bad at all, just a little tweak. An almost perfect match." He lifted them from her face and walked a few paces to a machine on the side.

The film, wall, whatever-it-was, had gone. She stared at his back. It looked like a perfectly ordinary, shirt-wearing back. She shifted in her seat. Maybe she'd imagined it. The light or something.

"Here." He turned round suddenly and held the glasses out.

Edee jumped and put them back on. The film-thing was there again.

"So, what's the verdict?" he asked after a second or two. "Change can be a strange beast. I'm sure you'll be used to them in no time. And glasses are very in these days. Thankfully. Such a welcome boost to business."

"Edee," said Mum again. "Are you going to say something? What do you think?"

"Er," said Edee.

"I do apologise, she's not usually—"

Seeing what-the-actual-what.

"—this inarticulate," said Mum.

"Here," said the optician. "Why don't you take a look at this and have a little read. You'll probably find even the tiniest font ever so clear."

She glanced down at the piece of card he was offering her. It was clear. It was also just a regular piece of card which, at that moment, was ridiculously awesome. "Yeah. Yeah, it is." She looked back at him. The film was still there, still covering him. There was a shimmering quality to it. A stripy shimmering that was more obvious when he moved. The stripes were vertical, running from his head to his feet. It looked . . . like a barcode. Like he was wrapped up in a see-through barcode.

Which was impossible. Obviously.

"Do they . . . they're just for astigmatism, right?" said Edee, meeting his eyes for the first time. His own glasses were round and brown.

"Yes, that's it. Well remembered. Corrects the oval nature of your eyes to reduce the blurriness. Or increase sharpness, whichever way you prefer to look at it."

"And nothing else?" said Edee.

"No, nothing else. Personally, I think the gift of sight is gift enough. Beyond that, our magical-powers range is a tad

4

limited at present." He laughed at his own joke and Edee searched his face. Was he lying?

"Let's have a proper look then," said Mum.

Edee carried on watching the optician as she turned her head in her mum's direction. He was smiling an indecipherable smile. It could be nothing. It could be creepy. It could be knowing. It was probably nothing.

"Yes," said Mum. "I see what you mean. They really do suit her."

Edee's eyes flicked to her mum and . . . and . . . whoa.

She shook her head, closed her eyes, and looked again. No way.

Her mum was wrapped up in a barcode too.

There was obviously something wrong with these lenses; they must've put some funny angle on them or got her prescription wrong or something. She took them off and glanced from her mum to the optician and back again. They both looked normal. She put the glasses back on and they were both covered—*encased*—by separate barcodes.

"Do the glasses ever go wrong?" asked Edee. "When they make them, the lenses, do they ever mess up? I mean, make them out of the wrong thing or . . . something?"

"Certainly not," said the optician. "When you come to an establishment like this, pay that little bit more, you are paying for quality."

He swivelled the chair to face the screen on the desk, like he'd finally had enough of this conversation. The shining barcode moved fluidly to fit his new form.

"Do you think they're faulty?" whispered Mum.

"I don't know," said Edee. "They're . . . not what I was expecting."

"They'll probably just take a bit of getting used to," said Mum.

"If you find you don't get on with them, which I'm sure

you will, but if you happen to be one of the very few who don't, you could always try contact lenses at some point," said the optician, still focusing on the screen. "Although there's more of an overhead cost-wise of course."

"Um, okay." Edee did not, right now, have the capacity to think about poking herself in the eye.

"Let's settle up then," said Mum, picking up her bag and standing. She sounded uncomfortable, like she really, really wanted to get out of here. Well, that was fine by Edee.

The optician reached to another part of the desk and held up a case. "This is for you. The cleaning cloth is inside."

"Thanks." She turned the case over. It must have made contact with the stripes but it looked normal. It looked like a glasses case.

"I'm multi-tasking today," said the optician, indicating the till with a flourish. He stood up and moved towards it. Mum followed.

The barcodes swished around both of them as they walked. Only 'swished' wasn't quite the right word because they looked so *there*. So solid. Like plastic wrapped around individual servings of meat in a chiller cabinet. Edee's stomach turned. What an image.

Mum rested her bag on the counter-top, pulled the zip, and took out her purse. She handed over her card. Moments later, she took the receipt and did everything in reverse until the bag was back on her shoulder.

The optician began straightening a few leaflets on the counter.

It was all so ordinary. Yet, covered by the stripes, none of it looked ordinary at all.

"Come on," said Mum.

Edee stood and moved slowly, as if the air itself had

doubled in density. What, exactly, had happened in the ⎙ twenty minutes?

"May you always be blessed with clarity of vision, or at least a clarity that can be fixed with some spectacles," said the optician. There was a smile in his voice. He held out a business card. "In case you'd like to recommend us. It's Jonathan. I should have told you that at the start."

"That was a peculiar thing to say," muttered Mum, as they shut the door. "Clarity of vision."

Maybe.

"Carmen's recommendations are usually spot on," said Mum, with a shake of her head. "Although the woman who tested your eyes last week was more normal."

"Mmm," said Edee.

Mum sighed. "I know you haven't had the easiest few weeks, but you still have to talk to people. It's no reason to be rude."

Edee pulled the glasses off and stuffed them into the case, before burying both the case and the card in her bag. "I wasn't. It was just a bit weird."

"You can say that again," said Mum.

She already was. WEIRD was circling around her brain as if her skull had been transformed into a velodrome. The only plus was that it had, however temporarily, disturbed the absent-Lucie fog that had been in place for fourteen long days.

2

"We just need a few bits. Do you want to stay here or come in?" said Mum, as they pulled into the supermarket car park.

"Stay here," said Edee.

"Anything you'd like?" said Mum.

"No," said Edee. Yes. Someone who could tell her what in the world had happened in the last half an hour.

Mum shut the door. Edee watched her walk across the car park before pulling out the glasses case. She flipped the lid and stared. They did look just like any other pair of glasses. She tapped the lenses. They felt like plastic. Normal plastic. Taking a deep breath, she held them in front of her eyes so she could see through them and around them at the same time.

She bit her lip.

There were five or six people milling about the car park. Even from this distance she could see that each one—*each one*—was covered by their own shining stripes. In the light of the overcast afternoon, they weren't as clear as they had been under the shop's light bulbs, but they were definitely there. It looked as if the light had to get through the what-ever-it-was to reach the person beyond. Inside.

She hooked the arms over her ears and watched the two people nearest to her. They were in the middle of a conversation. As they passed the windscreen, one took hold of the other's hand and their stripes butted up against each other. Edee leaned forward. A few steps later they were lost among the other cars. She sat back. The stripes hadn't joined or changed. They were separate. That's what it looked like.

She glanced down at her own hand.

Her stomach dropped.

She was looking at her normal, naked skin. She turned it one way, then the other. Nothing. She pulled down the sun shield and stared into the thin mirror. Nothing. No barcode. No shining.

It was a hand and a face unlike all the others.

Was that good or bad?

How could it be good? How could any of this be good?

Snapping the flap back up, she tugged the glasses from her face and dropped them onto the dashboard. Why was this happening? Didn't she already have enough different going on? More than enough. She balled her hands into fists, trying to stop them shaking. It didn't work. She pulled her phone from her bag instead. Message Lucie. That's what every cell in her body was demanding. Message Lucie, she would come over, and they'd figure this out together.

Except she wouldn't come over. She couldn't. Edee's eyes tingled again as she checked the time. It was pointless. If they were back in signal, Lucie would have messaged already. She'd have to tell her later.

Tell her *what*?

It might be nothing. She bit her lip a little harder. It wasn't nothing.

Opening a browser, her unsteady thumbs hovered above

the screen. What should she put? 'I can see lines around people' . . . 'When I put my glasses on, I can see something weird' . . . 'Do humans have barcodes?' . . . 'Can glasses have superpowers?'

She shook her head and started typing, then paused again. Because what if the answer, whatever it was, ended up being something she was better off not knowing? What if the barcode stuff . . . knew things?

The glasses on the dashboard seemed to double in size, like *they* might be the one who knew things. Edee stared. She could shove them back in her bag and forget about all of this. She could 'accidentally' drop them on the car park's tarmac. She really could see okay. And she really did not need this. Her hand went forward. But—

Something stopped her from picking them up.

Something niggling inside her. The barcodes were there. She'd seen them. She couldn't wipe the memory. She couldn't forget her naked hand. She couldn't. Her thumbs found the keyboard again.

———

At the thud of the boot, she looked up.

Her neck hurt.

Mum opened the driver-side door and slipped in. "I always forget how unpleasant supermarkets are." She clicked her seatbelt and started the engine. "Online shopping has to be the single greatest—"

Edee stopped listening. Nothing. There was nothing on the internet. But it was *the internet*. It had all the answers. To everything. Ever.

The closest, and it wasn't close at all, had been some skater in America who said he'd had a phase of seeing butterflies around people's heads. But it had only lasted two weeks and it had followed a concussion.

She had not had a concussion.

But . . . how could there be nothing on the internet?

She must've not searched the right thing. Things. Yet—

Mum nudged her leg.

"Huh?"

"I said I picked up some jacket potatoes for tea," said Mum. "Something easy."

"Okay," said Edee.

Mum took a breath like she was going to say something else, but she closed her mouth and flicked the indicator instead. Moments later she said, "Lots of people wear glasses. No one will notice after a week or two."

Edee said nothing. Her stomach had gripped because in this whatever-it-was, lots of people did not—apparently—have bodies without barcodes.

Mum sighed. Her knuckles turned a shade or two lighter around the steering wheel. "I know everything's different, Edee. And I wish more than anything that Rosa and Greg hadn't . . . " She audibly swallowed the end of the sentence.

Edee stared out of the window.

There was a pause.

"It will get easier," said Mum.

Edee jammed her tongue against her teeth. The absent-Lucie fog was back, and it was swirling with its new WEIRD companion around the knowledge—the certainty—that Mum would freak out at barcode shimmering. At Edee seeing things she couldn't . . . at Edee *seeing* things. She hadn't said anything in the optician's and now it was too late.

"You just need to make some new friends," said Mum.

If looks contained real power, the glass would have shattered. Not this again.

She had other friends. Cass and Maddie for starters. But that wasn't the point. The point was that the Lucie-shaped hole in her life could not just be plugged by them or by sheer numbers of people. And that was if she'd wanted it plugged in the first place. She didn't. She wanted her best friend back here, where she was supposed to be.

The one thing that was not going to happen.

Mum yawned then muttered, "I am so ready for the weekend."

The glasses slid along the dashboard in a weird crab-like movement as if they were expressing an opinion about Thursdays. Edee checked herself. Glasses were things and things definitely could not have an opinion. And yet . . .

She picked them up and held them between her finger and thumb.

"They aren't a toy," said Mum, a few moments later. "You saw how much they cost. Put them on for a bit and see if you can get used to them."

Edee folded the arms in and wrapped her fingers around the frames. By the time they got home the lenses were dotted with fingerprints.

3

Half an hour later, Mum was doing some work while the potatoes cooked and Edee (her mind a tiny bit clearer and her hands less shaky) was on the sofa and back to searching, because there had to be something. Something she had missed earlier.

Her eyes widened at the screen.

Auras. Could they be showing auras?

Except, how could a pair of glasses make you psychic? Yet it did say auras appeared around people. And maybe you couldn't see your own aura. That made sense. Maybe.

She glanced towards the doorway. If Mum caught her reading about auras she would flip out for sure. Keyboard sounds were coming from the office. She looked back to the screen and scanned a couple of articles.

'Electromagnetic energy' . . . 'an energy field' . . . 'layers' . . . 'luminous' . . . 'vibrations'.

Okay. What if it was? Lucie would think it was hilarious. She'd probably make her parents come back on a detour just so she could try them on. A tiny bubble of hope appeared in Edee's stomach. And popped. Even Lucie could not manage that.

'Everyone can see auras, they just need to try.'

What if the glasses bypassed the trying part? Maybe whoever had made the glasses had strong psychic ability and had somehow imbued them with it.

'Auras always tell you something.'

Something good? Something useful?

'Everything is made from energy, so everything has an aura: people, animals, plants, even non-living objects.'

Wait. Everything?

'Auras are seen as light, colours.'

There hadn't been colours, just shimmering.

She picked up the glasses from the arm of the sofa, put them on, and looked around the room. Her eyes came to rest on the towering plant in the corner that was making enormous pointed shadows on the wall. Nothing. It was just a plant. Leaves and stems and shadows. No shining stripes.

Dropping her phone to the sofa, she went to the window, opened one of the shutters, and peered down on the street. Two people were walking past. They were both covered by the shimmering stuff. Edee focused on the tree opposite: nothing. She looked to the cars parked at the side of the road: nothing. The lamp posts: nothing.

A person rounded the corner. They were walking a dog, and it was as clear as could be: the person was covered by the stuff but the dog wasn't. Edee watched until the edge of the building got in the way. Maybe the glasses only showed human auras. She frowned. Glasses that showed stuff but filtered it too? That didn't make sense. It couldn't be auras.

"What are you looking at?"

She spun round and recoiled at the sight of the shining barcode in the middle of the room.

Mum glanced up from straightening some magazines on the coffee table.

"I was . . . "

"Testing them out?" said Mum, nodding. "Let's have a go then."

Edee froze. What if Mum could see the lines? What if she couldn't? What if she realised her daughter didn't have them? What if she realised Edee hadn't said anything in the optician's?

Mum's hand was out. Expectant.

In slow motion, Edee took the glasses off and placed the frames in the upturned palm.

Mum was lifting them to her face.

She was moving her hair out of the way.

She was—

"Goodness." She stared at Edee, then down towards her own feet and around the room. "I mean . . . "

There was a dramatic, stretching pause.

"What?" said Edee. "Are you—"

"I didn't realise your eyesight was so bad," said Mum, her face falling. "I can't see a thing."

"What can you see?" Edee's voice caught in her throat. She coughed.

"A blurry mess of colours," said Mum. "There are no edges. No shapes." She held her hands out in front, as if to feel the way by patting the air, and turned towards the mirror on the chimney breast. "I can't even see what they look like." She raised the frames, scrunched up her eyes, and opened them again. "How can you function in life if you see this badly?" The lines on her forehead deepened. "How could I not have realised?"

"My sight isn't like that," said Edee, willing her voice to be normal. "It's that in reverse or something. I can see perfectly well without them."

"I think perfectly is something of an exaggeration." Mum moved towards the un-shuttered window, put the glasses back on, and looked one way down the street then the other.

Edee bent down and peered through the gap next to her mum's elbow. Two more people were moving along the pavement. "What can you see now?" She clasped her fingers to try and stop her hands feeling like enormous, awkward things that might tremble again at any moment.

"A much less colour-coordinated mess," said Mum. "Here." She took them off again and held them out. "You should have told me."

"I didn't know," said Edee. She hadn't. Just like she hadn't realised how much she'd relied on Lucie to read stuff on the board at school. The optician had said it would've been gradual.

"I had your eyes tested when you were little." Mum's brow creased a little more. "It was minor astigmatism then. They said it was nothing to worry about. There was never a follow-up appointment." She picked up the perfectly folded throw from the bucket chair, shook it out, and refolded it.

The glasses hung from Edee's hand. Mum was not going to let her off wearing the things. And—her body did a weird inwards contracting thing—there was no way to know if she had seen the stripes or not. Which meant . . . she still didn't know if *she* was seeing something weird through the lenses or whether the glasses were universally showing something weird. Did it matter? It had to. It was the difference between general weird and personal weird.

And that was on top of her lack of a barcode. The already-in-place personal weird. Her chest felt constricted, as if her lungs had forgotten how to work.

"Dinner's in five minutes," said Mum, gathering up a couple of old magazines. She stopped in the doorway, paused, then said, "You can tell me anything. I hope you know that."

Edee's non-moving, oxygen-deprived body ran cold. Had Mum seen them after all? No. She would have said. She meant tell her about the blurriness.

Mum hovered a moment longer. Edee couldn't think of anything to say. Mum disappeared into the kitchen.

Her phone on the sofa lit up.

Edes, I have to see your glasses. Now! AMAZING DAY. We hiked up a mountain. I swear it was a mountain. Had lunch at this place. It was practically hanging over the side. Amazing! xxxx

There was a picture of Lucie and her parents sat around a table with an unfamiliar kind of landscape behind them. They all looked happy. More than happy. Unfairly happy.

It was a perfectly landed punch.

A second message arrived. *PS miss youuuuuuuu xxx*

Edee's belly tied in a hundred knots. She shoved the glasses on, took a photo, threw the glasses to the sofa, and sent the thing with the most incongruous message she had ever typed. *Awesome! Cafe looks unreal. Can't believe you climbed a mountain while I had double maths and the optician's xxx*

Stuffing the phone in her pocket, she turned her back on the lounge. This time, no amount of gritted teeth could stop the tears from coming. She pressed her palms over her face. To her it was not PS I miss you. There was nothing PS about it. It was I *miss* you, nothing is the same, and I hate that this has happened.

It was also I need you.

The knots twisted and tugged.

4

Sleep was an evasive thing that night. Lucie sent a few more texts:

LOVE the glasses. Looks like you were meant to wear them. I never realised.

New campsite tomorrow and another hike, whoop! Who knew hiking was so much fun?

Dad's playing guitar with the people in the camper van next to us. Hahaha. He's terrible. They're worse.

Several times Edee started writing about glasses and lines but nothing felt right. Instead, she sent pointless comments about the things Lucie mentioned. It felt so clunky, so wrong.

Eventually the screen stayed dark, and Edee stared at the matching black ceiling while her brain went over and over the afternoon and evening. At some point she must have fallen into a restless half-sleep because, soon enough, her alarm was pulling her back to the room and her bleary eyes strayed magnetically to the glasses case on the shelf. The mass of knots returned. Her heartbeat quickened. Maybe today the glasses would just be glasses and none of the other stuff would matter. Please. She closed her eyes again for a second. *Please.*

Her hand reached for the case. Her fingers curled around it . . . then she swung herself out of bed and shoved it into her bag.

Thirty minutes later, she was on the way to the bus stop while a niggling voice in her head was telling her that she could've tried them on a hundred times already. It wasn't as if she hadn't had time. The old schedule, the one that left time to meet Lucie on the corner and have a slow, chatty walk, was etched on to her brain. For the last two weeks it had meant a dragging wait at the bus stop. Today, she could not bear it. Slowing for a second or two, she headed right past and carried on walking. She'd rather be late.

The route took her away from the noise of the car and bus commute and into the park. The place was full of runners, dog walkers, and walking commuters.

People, people, people.

Her stomach somersaulted.

She could not put it off any longer.

Pulling the glasses from her bag, she shoved them onto her face. The effect was immediate. Glittering lines lit up the park like someone had inserted a layer across, in front of, around, normal.

It was not normal.

Ripping the frames from her face again, the scene became ordinary—exactly as it had in the optician's. Raising them to her face once more, the lines returned. She glanced at her other hand. It was still naked.

Her body felt like it belonged to someone else. Except she'd known. Deep down she had. Yesterday hadn't been some kind of one-off quirk. The glasses—the personalised prescription glasses—were showing *her* this thing.

Why?

Because this was the worst year ever? Because she just didn't have enough weird to be getting on with? Because she'd won some sort of weird lottery?

She shook her head a tiny, imperceptible amount. The hand that was wrapped around the lenses dropped to her side.

A man swung past from behind and tutted, as if she had chosen to stop there with the express intention to annoy him. But, by the time the tut had fully registered in Edee's brain, he was far along the path hurrying to wherever it was he needed to be.

"Everything alright?" asked a woman. She was pushing a pram and heading away from the tutting man. "You look like you've seen a ghost."

"Yeahfinethanks," said Edee, shoving the glasses away and starting to move again while wishing for the first time in her life that she had seen a ghost. A ghost would've been easier to understand. It would've been a ghost. The lines were . . . what? What were they for? What did they do? Why didn't she have any? Her heartbeat thudded, her stomach tightened, and she jammed her tongue into her teeth.

———

"Did you miss the bus?" said Cass, leaning forward as Edee, head down, slipped into the seat next to Maddie. Cass, as usual, had taken the one by the wall.

Trying to be as inconspicuous as possible, Edee shook her head. Mr Lewin had clocked her coming in and she was sure he was still watching her. That was another thing about Lucie's absence. Somehow it had twisted the spotlight her way. Mrs Obee had actually stopped her at the end of Monday's English class, after making them work in pairs, and said how difficult it must be. She'd said it like something terrible had happened—not that Lucie had started the world's longest holiday—and Edee had felt awful for thinking maybe it was worse because Lucie was out there yet nothing, nothing, nothing was the same. She'd clamped her mouth shut and Mrs Obee had eventually moved off.

She slumped further into the seat, to take better cover behind the back of Errol Green. She wished he was twice as broad.

Cass leaned forward a little more.

"I walked," Edee muttered.

"Walked?" Maddie screwed up her nose as if it were the strangest thing anyone could've done. Yet, without waiting for an explanation, she added, "Did you see the cafe?"

Edee managed to nod.

"Lucie's so lucky." Cass leaned on her elbows, tilting her chair onto the front legs. "I wish I had her parents."

"We're going to have to come up with some seriously good pictures," said Maddie. "It's only week two and she's killing it."

"Pictures of what?" said Cass. "We've got school and the park. They're boring."

"We'll just have to get creative," said Maddie. "Oh!" She grabbed Cass's arm.

Edee ducked even lower as Mr Lewin looked over.

"We should edit ourselves into her pictures," said Maddie.

"What?" said Cass.

"She uploads one," said Maddie, "and we upload one of her other ones but with us in it too."

Cass nodded a little. "That would be funny." She slumped backwards, her chair thudding on the thin carpet. "But not as good as being there for real. How is it fair that her parents gave her amazing genes and they take her out of school to go off round the world?"

"Europe, you mean." Maddie screwed her nose up again. "And they're living in a *caravan*."

"A camper van," said Cass. "And so what? She's seeing new stuff every day while we're stuck here, where nothing ever happens."

The knots in Edee's stomach pulled so tight they hurt.

Maddie's whole face screwed up this time. "She's got no space, and no stuff, and she's practically sharing a room with her parents. It's weird. You think it's weird, don't you, Edes?"

"Yeah," said Edee. Everything was weird.

Cass shrugged and crossed her arms on the desk. "She's out there and we're stuck here. Whatever way you look at it she's winning. I've never seen people smile like that. They were grins with eyes."

Edee winced. That was the point. The exact gut-wrenching point she had been trying to ignore for days.

Lucie was loving it.

She was loving it even though she hadn't wanted to go; even though she'd insisted there was no way miles would get in the way of them being best friends. Yet all it had taken was a few days and she was revelling in new and different while Edee was drowning in it. Not only was she drowning, but her version of new and different had been hijacked by some kind of magic glasses that had launched new and different to a whole other stratosphere. No. They hadn't launched her. They were pulling her downwards, sucking her towards the stratosphere on the other side of the planet.

And that's why she hadn't told Lucie.

And . . . that's why she had to figure this out.

Her whole body contracted. It was right, she had to because . . . she did not want to be the one who was drowning; the one who kept having to fight her own tear ducts; the one who was under surveillance. And because . . . what if it wasn't one thing after another—Lucie leaving and *then* the glittering? What if the two things were a back and a front of the same thing and solving one would solve the other? Was that possible?

She closed her eyes for a second or two. How could it be? And yet her bag was vibrating against her foot as if it were agreeing. More likely it was Lucie's daily text telling them to let her know every single thing that happened today, as if things were normal. Her skin goose-bumped. New, unasked for, inescapable, abnormal. That's what it was.

5
___

Their first class was history, and Mr Millard was droning on about primary sources. At least he probably still was. Edee had stopped listening. The glasses were back on her face and her bag was on her lap under the desk. It was shielding her phone and she was scrolling through photos because Lucie did have lines. The more unexpected news—the news that had captured her unswerving attention for the last few minutes, but had somehow escaped her last night—was that the lines showed up in photos.

It shouldn't have been shocking (they were around the people after all) yet it was. Everything about the pictures was familiar and it wasn't at the same time. Like this morning. Like yesterday afternoon.

She scrolled back past her birthday, past Lucie's, and back through the summer. There were loads of photos at Lucie's with the place getting more and more full through the timeline. In between there were others: the barbecue at Maddie's, afternoons in the park, the weekend the three of them had stayed at Lucie's, the Saturday they'd stayed at hers. Lines, lines, lines.

She stared a little harder and brought the phone a fraction closer. They changed. That's what it looked like. In different pictures of the same person, different bits of the barcode were glowing. Was that right? She zoomed in on a picture of Lucie. There were shining lines over her left side. She scrolled forwards through a few more to one she'd noticed of them in the park because, yes, on that one there were bright lines over her face. They were so bright you wouldn't necessarily realise it was her. One picture was inside and one was outside. Could that be the difference? No, because she had been recognisable in other outside photos. So, different parts of the barcode glowed and glittered at different times then?

The lines on the photos didn't pick up on the glittering though. They looked like single strips of light. If she had only seen the photo, she would have had no idea about the scale of the thing. The luminescence. And no idea that they looked alive. Alive. Wait. Her breath caught. That was exactly right. But if they looked alive, then what did it mean if you were without them?

The room was in silence. She realised a moment too late.

Mr Millard was standing beside the desk with his hands crossed in some sort of pointed display of fake patience. He was looking—leering—at the screen in her hand. Twenty-eight glittering faces were turned her way. Twenty-six of them looked like they couldn't believe their luck at this turn of events. Cass, it turned out, was nudging her leg.

Edee's face warmed again. The attention pressed on her. Like *it* was alive.

"She's got glasses," muttered someone.

"Not strong enough," whispered someone else, sniggering.

"There's nothing to see here. Carry on," said Mr Millard, raising a hand, as if he hadn't been the one drawing attention to it in the first place.

A few people lowered their heads. A few chairs creaked. No one went back to work.

Edee turned her phone over and slipped it into her bag.

Mr Millard shifted his position from one foot to the other. "Edee, are you aware of the invisibility policy?"

Her face raced through warm to hot. It was only two weeks into the term. She hadn't been entirely sure he had known her name. He was new. The only teacher who hadn't been holding her under surveillance. She moved her head downwards in half a nod.

"I thought it would have been quite something to have slipped your attention," he said. The sarcasm oozed. There were flyers plastered over every noticeboard in the place and splashed across the canteen. "So, would you like to enlighten me as to the necessity of looking at photos in this class?"

Someone else snickered.

Edee said nothing.

"Really," said Mr Millard. "I'm curious. It might help me to prepare lessons that would be more . . . engaging for you."

"Her best friend has moved away," said Maddie.

"I'm aware of that," said Mr Millard. The words were clipped. His tone was sharp.

Edee slipped a little down her seat.

"However," he continued, "as far as I'm aware, the policy does not say that phones must be invisible unless a student wishes to communicate with an absent friend. Am I correct?"

She nodded again.

"I didn't quite catch that," said Mr Millard.

"Yes," said Edee, concentrating on the table. Part of her was grateful to Maddie for speaking up. Another, larger part, wished she hadn't. She wanted Mr Millard to move out of her space. Aside from everything else, the glittering radiating from his body was hurting her eyes.

"Detention. Here. Twelve-thirty," said Mr Millard. "And if I see it again, it will be confiscated. If temptation is too great, I suggest you leave it in your locker."

Edee's face had never felt so hot. Her hands were clammy—her whole body was—and her eyes were smarting, yet she did not stop watching as he moved away. His back might have been crackling with all the light coming from it.

"A piece of advice," he said, addressing the class who were at various levels of openness in their continued watching. "Two words that will serve you well for the future." He paused. "Eye contact."

His glittery barcode had notched up another level. Edee tore the glasses from her face. He met her eyes. She looked away.

"I CAN'T BELIEVE he did that," said Maddie, glancing over her shoulder. The bell had gone for the end of the lesson and they'd filed out into the corridor. "What a control freak."

"I can't believe you told him about Lucie," said Cass. "I thought you were going to get detention as well. For sure."

Maddie hoisted her bag onto her shoulder. "Anyone normal would've said to put it away, not make a massive scene."

"What were you looking at anyway?" said Cass. "I was kicking you so hard your leg's going to be a mess."

Another classroom emptied into the corridor. Edee let a couple of people jostle in front of her before catching up. "Photos."

"Lucie's?" Cass pushed past a line of year sevens. "You looked like you were about to climb into your phone."

She half nodded and heard herself say, "I was thinking about editing them. Like Maddie said."

"So was I," said Maddie. The three of them turned into their English classroom. "I just didn't get my phone out."

Edee slipped into the seat next to Cass. The empty one on the other side seemed like a yawning, cavernous thing.

"It's like Lucie said, isn't it?" said Maddie, taking a mirror from her bag and moving her face side to side. "About being smart. We've got to be here, but they can't know what we're thinking about."

Edee stared into her open bag, forgetting what she was supposed to be taking from it. Lucie had said that. Her parents had said it to her in the weeks before they'd quit their jobs; that your mind was yours. It had seemed like nothing then—they'd been reading loads of books and getting enthusiastic about all sorts of ideas and people for months—but now it was obvious. Everything, all the changes, had amped up from that exact moment.

Her hand nudged the glasses case. Mr Millard's sarcasm burned again.

Maybe it was a better point than she'd realised. Or, rather, it was relevant right now. He could dish out detention, and any teacher could threaten to confiscate her phone, but none of them would confiscate her glasses. She was going to be around people all day. She was in a laboratory.

Her stomach turned. No, not that. It was just convenient. And practical. Because she had to. Because how else was she going to figure this out? She put the case on the desk.

Cass picked it up. "I forgot you were getting these. Why didn't you show us? They look amazing." She took them out and put them on. "You're so lucky."

Edee bit her lip. And watched.

Cass glanced to the window behind. "What do you reckon? Do they suit me?"

"Sure." Maddie passed across the mirror. "But they look better on Edes."

"Her face is bigger," said Cass. She glanced in the mirror, then out across the classroom and towards the corridor. "I can't see much."

"Mum said the same," muttered Edee. And, just like her, Cass had shown nothing out of the ordinary. No raised eyebrows. No pauses. No 'what!' expression.

She was now sliding the frames down her nose and rotating her head, eyes on the mirror. "I think I'd suit rounder ones, maybe. I'm going to tell Mum I need mine tested again." She took them off and handed them back as if they were an ordinary, sight-correcting apparatus.

Edee hesitated for a moment before putting them back on. The glittery world returned. What if she told them about it, right now? She could. It would be easy, a few words, a minute or two. They could help her figure it out.

Her lips pressed together. No.

She was the one who'd become the third of three, not one-quarter of a four. And *they* had lines. Besides, if she was under surveillance for Lucie going, then all hell would break out at glittering lines should any of the teachers overhear. And she needed that like, well, a world full of glittering lines.

Maddie leaned in. Her hand began moving towards the

29

glasses, then recoiled, as a shining Mrs Obee rushed into the room telling them they had a mountain to get through in the next hour. Edee's fingers pressed against the frames. It would be so easy to hook them round and pull the things off. She did not. She could not. The little voice from earlier was back. What if this did have something to do with Lucie leaving? It was stupid, of course it was. Rationally, it was beyond stupid. And yet her fingers did not move.

A couple of hours later her eyes were aching. It might've been because of the intensity of the light coming from all directions (which made sense) or because of the continual sharpness (which didn't; the whole point of the glasses was supposed to be sharpness). Either way, she made herself keep wearing them through the detention—this time as a protest—while Mr Millard droned on and on about the origins of the invisibility policy, as if it were some ancient relic. She focused on the place just above his ears, and tried to squint as little as possible as his barcode sent out enough light to illuminate a small country.

As soon as he said she was free to go, however, she turned around and ripped them off. The world un-glittered and seemed extra blurry. She felt a peculiar kind of flat. In the last three hours, all she'd seen was that people were covered by barcodes that glittered and changed. She'd known that before. But why? She massaged the sides of her head. It wasn't going to be easy, of course it wasn't.

6

By the time she walked up the stairs to their apartment later that afternoon, Edee was craving some downtime. The eye-ache had eased but it was lurking, as if it would swoop back down given the smallest opportunity. She paused at the top of the landing and pulled the glasses from her bag once more. Mum's car had been in their space. If she wore them in (and Mum came out of her office) she could tell her that her eyes needed a rest. It was true. Her brain needed a rest. That was more true. She was going to lie on the sofa and not think about any of it until dinner.

Turning the key and pushing the door, she faltered. There were three unfamiliar pairs of shoes scattered by the rack. One was large, one was medium, and one was tiny. The tiny ones barely counted as shoes.

Her fingertips lingered on the handle while her senses double checked that this was, in fact, their home. They never had unplanned visitors. Well, almost never. Besides, who did Mum know with a baby? And why today? She shut her eyes for a moment. Why, why, why.

The door slipped and thudded shut. She winced, then strained to hear the conversation coming from the lounge. If they hadn't heard the thud, she might be able to head to her room and—

Mum appeared at the other end of the hallway. "There you are. Good day?"

Edee made a sound that might've meant yes or no. She twisted sideways and busied herself with her own shoes. Even after all the barcodes she'd seen today, this one was just as jarring as it had been yesterday. Maybe more so. It was Mum-not-Mum in their hallway of unfamiliar shoes. She bit her lip.

"You remember Craig, don't you?" continued Mum. "He used to work at Veronica's. Craig Leigh."

"Mmm," said Edee towards the floorboards. She knew the name. They'd met once or twice. She did not, right now, feel any sort of need to talk to him. Unless he could help her make sense of all this and, given she was not going to tell him, that was not going to happen.

"I popped into town on the way home," said Mum. "And bumped into him. Scotty and Amber are here too. Come and say hello."

Edee put her shoes on the rack, let her bag thud to the ground, and, for perhaps the billionth time, wished she were Lucie. Not for the living in a camper van, moving away part, but for the saying what you thought part. If she were Lucie, she would just say no. Then she'd go to her room, come out when she wanted to, and no one would get upset about it.

Except that wasn't right. That would be if she could somehow be Lucie and also still be herself. Because if real-Lucie were here, she would actually be skipping down the hallway like a gazelle. Lucie loved new people.

Her stomach lurched. Maybe that's why she loved the

travelling. Maybe she should have known it was going to turn out that way. Maybe she had and that's why saying goodbye had been so hard.

Mum cleared her throat. She was holding out a hand, like some kind of illuminated tour guide.

Edee closed her eyes for a moment then trudged along the hall. Perhaps she could say about the headache. Perhaps she could—

A cartoon-like gasp almost escaped from her mouth at the scene before her; at the level of weird that was occupying their lounge. It was too much to absorb in one go. Way, way too much. It was . . . half of the sofa looked like it was on fire. Someone—it had to be Craig—was sitting there but the lines covering his body were so bright they practically made a screen. She squinted, desperate to shield her eyes, and looked away.

Scotty was sitting in the bucket chair, phone in hand. He was also surrounded by a barcode. It was active, glittering away, but nowhere near as bright as his dad's.

Her mum, now standing to the side, opposite Craig, was covered in the same kind of glittering as a moment ago; except a strip, going down over her front, right over her heart, was glowing. It might have been an arrow pointing to the unequivocal proof that the barcodes *did* change, but Edee barely stopped to consider that because her eyes had found Amber. The little girl . . . had nothing.

Nothing.

She was the only other person in the last twenty-four hours who had not been covered.

Edee's mind whirled. She was . . . whatever *this* was . . . had put her in the same group (category?) as a baby? No. That was . . . wrong.

The gasp in her throat turned into a constriction. She

swallowed once, twice. There must be a mistake. She was nothing like a baby. She was fifteen.

"Edee?" Mum sounded like she was talking from the end of a long, anti-acoustic corridor, but it was enough to wrench her attention back to the room.

Mum was frowning.

"Um," managed Edee. "Hi."

Scotty nodded to her. He looked about as impressed to be here as she'd felt minutes ago. He also looked completely out of place among the throws and the cushions. It was too ordinary a thing to notice.

"Nice to see you again," said Craig.

The words were incongruous with his tone and with the shining. His voice sounded empty.

Edee shut her eyes once more and raised the glasses to the top of her head. Maybe he was sick. He'd looked like a person-sized sun. If the lines had been heat as well as light, he would be frying.

She clamped her jaw shut. She felt sick.

And yet . . . without the glasses, the scene looked ordinary. Out of place, but ordinary. Ordinary enough. Just downbeat.

She found herself looking back at Amber. The little girl had plopped to sitting. Her pudgy nappy was skewing the proportions of her small body, and she was gazing up at Edee as if she were the most interesting thing in the world. A drop of dribble was hanging from her tiny chin.

Edee pulled her sleeves over her hands and entwined her fingers in the cuffs.

"We were just saying how long it's been since Craig and Scotty have been here," said Mum. "We think it must be eight, nine years. Too long at any rate. You were both at primary school, in the infants." She wafted her hand in a strange, un-Mum-like way. "Anyway, I was just going to make some drinks. Craig, why don't you help me?"

The man seemed caught in a number of minds. He opened and closed his mouth, went to stand, then stopped and glanced over to Scotty. "Will you watch her?"

Scotty, not looking up from the screen nor moving from the chair, gave a single nod of his head.

Craig stood, hesitated again, then headed to the hallway.

There was a moment or two of silence. Amber gave a dribbling grin. She giggled. It seemed utterly out of place.

"She does that," said Scotty, raising his eyes from the phone.

Edee freed her fingers and shoved her hands in her pockets.

Amber flopped forwards and began crawling.

Edee pulled her hands from her pockets. This was their living room and she did not know what to do with herself. She knelt down. Something squeaked. She pulled a squashy, plastic giraffe from under her knee.

"She gnaws on that," said Scotty.

Edee dropped it and awkwardly moved to sitting. "What's going on? I mean . . ."

"How come we've ended up here?" said Scotty. "Spreading the joy."

The unexpectedness of his tone, the frankness of it, hit her like a solid thing. It was such a relief to hear someone else acknowledge a weirdness. Any weirdness. Had she been a different person (Lucie) she might have run over and hugged him. Instead, she said, "Yeah."

"My mum's left him," said Scotty. It was matter-of-fact this time, as if he were describing a sandwich he'd had for lunch. "We were in town. Dad was standing in the street not moving. Your mum saw us."

"Right."

Amber had halted. She was giving another salivary grin.

"She didn't get the email," said Scotty.

For a moment Edee wasn't sure if he meant his mum, her mum, or Amber.

"She's lucky," muttered Scotty. He flicked a squashy, multi-coloured ball with his toe. It rolled to a stop by the baby, who laughed.

"Where's she gone?" said Edee.

"Moved in with the graphic designer at Dad's work two days ago," said Scotty. "It's been a pretty awesome week."

Edee nodded slowly. That was for sure.

"Yours too?" said Scotty.

She began to nod then stopped. It didn't seem right to compare hers to what he'd just said. Except, yes. "It's been weird."

"Good or bad?" said Scotty.

"I don't know," said Edee.

He gave a wry smile. "You've got randoms in your place on a Friday evening. I think that's a clue."

She nodded again and, with immense understatement, said, "It's been unexpected, I guess."

"Tell me about it," said Scotty. "Mum didn't run her plans past me first."

She almost smiled then said, "Sorry."

He gave a kind of face-shrug. "Makes a change from blank faces and crying."

Amber was chewing on the soft ball now. The fabric had darkened.

"Mum keeps phoning and crying," said Scotty. "But she's the one who left. And Dad cries when he thinks we're asleep." He scuffed his socked foot across the rug. "Parents are weird."

If only it were limited to parents.

Scotty held his phone between his thumb and first finger and rotated it against his leg. "He's called Reg. He's Scottish. So that's a bit awkward."

It was deadpan. He smiled. So did she.

She could tell the adults were coming back by the way it evaporated from his lips and his attention returned to his phone.

7

They left just before six. Mum headed downstairs to see them off. Edee headed to her room, pulling the glasses back onto her face, and watching out the window. Craig's barcode was shining just as brightly, and Scotty's was also similar to a couple of hours ago. The lines over Mum's heart had dulled a little and Amber was still uncovered.

Considering the *different* out there, the last hour and a half had been surprisingly uneventful. In fact, it had been nothing. Mum and Craig had spent it reminiscing about the people they used to work with (or rather Mum had talked and Craig had sat there looking lost and chipping in now and again) while Scotty had concentrated on his phone most of the time. If it hadn't been for the baby, Edee would've used the headache excuse and left. Instead, of course, she'd spent the time trying to figure out any way in which she could be similar to the person who could not yet walk and talk. She had not come up with a single thing. At least, nothing beyond the fact that she had once been a baby too. But so had everyone.

Except, wait . . . genes.

She stepped back from the window. What if no lines was somehow genetic? Perhaps Scotty had inherited his lines from Craig, and Amber had inherited no lines from their mum. Edee might have inherited no lines from her dad.

She reached the other side of her room with a few quick strides and pushed the door closed while pulling her phone from her bag. Ignoring the messages from Lucie and the others, as well as her own galloping heart, she scrolled to Dad's number and zoomed in on his face.

The zoom was unnecessary. There were lines everywhere.

But hang on. You could inherit something from recessive genes too, like blue eyes from brown-eyed parents. She opened a browser. Scotty's mum was called . . . Jo. She'd worked for the web designer that had been in the same building as Mum's old job (what a random thing to have stayed in her brain). There she was. The same eyes and nose as Scotty.

And the same lines too. No, not the same. But there.

Everything plummeted. Could both she and Amber have some kind of rare recessive gene? It seemed unlikely. For the umpteenth time, Edee looked at her own un-glittering body. She slumped onto her bed.

And froze. Amber's mum had left. Could it be that? A leaving parent somehow sucked away the lines?

Except Scotty's lines were there and his mum had left both of them. Then again, Scotty was older. Maybe it was a parent leaving when you were a baby thing. Could it be? How? They took a part of you with them? No, surely not.

But her dad and Amber's mum had both left.

She worried a nail. First her dad and now Lucie. Was she just someone that other people left? What if that was the connection? What if they could somehow sense something was missing and didn't want to stay around?

Except . . . Dad had never really left. Not like Lucie. You couldn't leave if you'd never been around. And, however much Lucie was loving everything now, she hadn't chosen to go either.

Edee rubbed the sides of her head.

How was she supposed to figure this out? Why would the glasses show her this stuff without providing any clues about what it was? What was the point?

The front door clicked shut.

"I'm going to throw some pasta together for tea," said Mum from the hallway. There was a pause. "Okay?"

"Mmm," said Edee.

There was another pause, then the door began opening, and Mum's shimmering face appeared in the gap followed by the rest of her as she kept on pushing. "I hope you didn't mind them coming over. Craig looked so lost in town I couldn't just leave them."

Some of the lines over her heart were glittering again. Why? How? Edee's fingers were still at the sides of her head.

Mum was watching.

She lowered them.

Mum crossed her arms over her chest and leaned on the doorframe. The lines still glowed. "It's hard to believe she's left them."

Parents are weird. Edee heard it in Scotty's voice, as if he had materialised in the room right then (and *that* would've been the definitive proof the world had gone crazy). Maybe people were weird. And some were more weird than others. She jammed her tongue into her teeth and pushed the glasses back up onto her head.

Un-lined Mum took a few steps into the room and sat

on the edge of the bed. "Listen, I've been thinking about something for a while and seeing Craig today has made up my mind."

Craig? What did Craig have to do with anything?

"It was the reason I was in town in the first place, actually," said Mum. "I want you to speak to a counsellor."

Whatever Edee might have been expecting, it was not that. "What?"

"I want you to see a counsellor," said Mum. "I think it would be helpful."

Because Craig's wife had left him?

"One's been recommended to me," said Mum. "A couple of times, actually." Her face was consumed by such an intense look. It was like . . . another layer of surveillance. "So many people I know have found it useful and wished they'd spoken to someone when they were younger. I don't see the point in waiting, letting a problem fester."

Edee's stomach, that had, she realised then, been surprisingly calm for a while, found a whole new way to twist and churn.

"I want to give you the opportunity to talk through things with someone neutral," continued Mum. "Someone who can offer a fresh perspective."

"On what?" said Edee. The only person she wanted to talk to was someone who could throw some light on the barcodes. And only if they brought it up first.

"On things that might be worrying you," said Mum. "Friendships, for example."

It was beginning to sound like a rehearsed speech.

Mum was still watching.

"I'm not worried about that," Edee managed. She wasn't. It was Mum who thought she needed to have hundreds of friends. She had Cass and Maddie. And when

41

she figured this out, maybe she'd have Lucie again. Proper Lucie.

"I should have done something before now," said Mum. "Then perhaps Lucie going away wouldn't have hit you so hard."

Edee's throat tightened. "It wasn't her fault."

"I know," said Mum. "She's a lovely girl. It's just an example."

"Of what?" said Edee.

"Being too dependent on one person," said Mum. "I want you to be independent. Confident."

Edee looked away for a moment. "I don't want to see a counsellor."

There was a moment or two before Mum replied. "It's not up for discussion."

"But . . ." Seeing a counsellor was not up for discussion? Wasn't that the world's biggest irony?

"She has a space on Monday afternoon. I'll email her and confirm," said Mum. "She's called Maggie. She comes highly recommended."

Edee's body felt light, unreal. Counselling. Monday. No, she had enough going on. More than enough.

"I'm doing this for you because I love you and I think it's best," said Mum. "You won't talk to me about it and I . . . well, it's not about me. I have to accept I can't be everything for you either, and neither should I be. This is an investment in your future. You have exams next year."

Exams? What did exams have to do with friends? With anything? Edee bit her lip. This whole conversation felt like something that had happened in someone else's life, not one spoken by real lips in real air in her bedroom.

For the simple lack of knowing what else to do, she dropped the glasses to her face. Mum's lines were doing a good job of impersonating Craig's. She pulled them off. No. Bad, bad idea. Not now. Not right now.

Mum stood up. "I'm going to make a start on dinner." She took a piece of paper from her fist. It had been lodged behind her thumb. She put it on the duvet and walked towards the doorway. "That's Scotty's phone number. I think he could do with some support."

Edee stared at the piece of paper. Mum was sending her to counselling, and now she was telling her she should be some kind of what—emotional support?—for a boy she'd spoken to for the first time in years? This was unreal. It had to be unreal. Except the duvet was crumpled where Mum had been sitting, there was a piece of paper by her side with a phone number on it, and the door was closing.

How was it even possible that the weirdest twenty-four hours in history had notched up another level? She felt empty as well as light, as if every piece of energy had been sucked from her body. Even the knots and the tightness had given up.

Another update flashed up on her screen. Another photo. More grins with eyes. She flipped the phone over. No one would send Lucie to counselling. And if Lucie were still here, Mum wouldn't be doing this. How had everything changed so quickly from something, two things, that she had not asked for?

8

The next morning, Edee woke to the buzzing and buzzing of her phone. Half-raising her eyelids, she retrieved the thing from the floor, pushed her hair out her face, and flopped back onto the pillow. "Hello."

"Yay!" said Lucie. "You're awake. Bonjour."

Yesterday flooded Edee's mind: the park, detention, Amber, counselling. She rolled onto her side as if she could roll away from it all.

"Did I sound like a local?" said Lucie.

"Yeah," said Edee.

"Mum and Dad are running," said Lucie. "They wanted me to go too, but I wanted to talk to you. It feels like forever."

It really, really did. And the face on the screen was glowing. Happy. Edee's eyes tingled. No. She was not going there.

"I've got so much to tell you," continued Lucie. "And I want to hear everything."

Edee rubbed her face. "You go first. I mean, here's here."

Lucie turned sideways and propped her phone on her knees. "It's so weird that everything is still going on there even though we're here. I want to be in two places at once. Edes, imagine if you could. You could be here too. How amazing would that be?"

It would. If only the glasses could've shown her that instead. Something useful.

"Do you reckon your mum would let you come for a visit?" said Lucie. "This sofa's a bed. There's loads of room. Look." She held the phone at arm's length. "It would be awesome. We've met so many amazing people already. I'm going to start filming stuff properly so you can all meet them too." She laughed. "Can you believe I get to do that as school?"

Edee shook her head.

"And Dad's decided we've got to use these," said Lucie, holding up a stack of scruffy paper maps. "He told me it was history and geography in one. So far we've got lost every day but we've also found these amazing places by accident, so he thinks he's a genius. You know the cafe, the one that—"

Edee let the words wash over her. If she zoned out a little bit from the specifics, then almost it could be the way it was. The enthusiasm. The Lucieness. It was all so familiar.

Lucie was laughing again. Edee couldn't help herself and smiled too. But it wasn't right. Everything was different. She glanced to the open glasses case.

"Let's see your glasses."

Edee started. No. Coincidence, that was all. She reached across to her bedside shelf and held them up.

"I want to try them so bad," said Lucie, leaning forward. "Put them on. I've got to see them properly."

Edee steeled herself, slipped them onto her face, and did

her best to ignore the real-time lines that glittered around her friend.

"They look so good," said Lucie, tilting her head. "It's like you were meant to wear glasses."

Edee bit her lip.

The face in the screen, behind the lines, shone and Edee almost told her everything right then, but she hesitated, and Lucie was swivelling her head and beckoning. "Hey, Mum, come and see Ede's glasses."

A sweaty and glittering Rosa appeared in the picture. She waved. "Hi Edee. Oh, wow, they do suit you. Lucie said they did."

Edee's heartbeat thudded. She tried to smile. It felt more like a grimace.

"How are you?" said Rosa. "How's your mum?"

"Yeah, fine," managed Edee, wanting to look away and for more than the shining. Rosa had been the one who'd propelled these changes. All of this had been her idea.

"Great," said Rosa. "What do you think of our new place? Have you had the guided tour now it's finished?"

"Not yet," said Lucie. She swung her legs over the side of the sofa and her mum went out of the picture. "I'm going to do a proper video, but you can get the preview. Because you're Edes." She stood, swept the camera across to her dad, who waved (also glittering), then pointed it back on her own face. "Are you alright? You look a bit—"

"Fine," said Edee quickly. Lucie was the one person she would tell, but not yet. Not with her parents there and not while Lucie seemed so full of everything and not until she knew just a little bit more. "It's just . . . crazy that you're so far away."

"I know, right?" said Lucie. "And it isn't even that far. Not really." The picture bobbed as she moved down a couple of steps. "This is our front door." She pushed it closed, then opened it again. "Oh, wait. Let me show you where we are first." She turned and flipped the picture. The screen filled with out-of-focus green. "Hang on." She tilted the camera and the green became a triangular incline of trees. The point was in the centre of the picture and a rocky hillside lifted in a wonky kind of reflection. The middle section was filled by a deep blue sky. "You can tell it's a different country though, can't you." She held the picture steady for a bit, then lowered it again and panned once more. "The shower block's over there. They've got these composting loos. They haven't got a flush. Then over there is the—"

"Wait," said Edee. She leaned in.

The picture stuttered backwards.

"What?" said Lucie.

A family was passing by. Two adults, an older child, and a toddler. Edee leaned closer, as if she really was trying to pass through the glass. Three of them, the adults and the older child, were covered in the glittering. The small one was not. Wait. Was that another coincidence? But . . . how could it be? Anybody could have been passing by right then.

"What?" said Lucie again. "What can you see?"

"Nothing," said Edee. "I . . . nothing. I mean, just that baby. It's, um, cute."

"Baby?" said Lucie. "Really? What have you done with Edes?" She laughed. "I suppose it's cute. There are tons here." She panned the camera a little further to the left. "There's a play area over there."

The family walked out of shot.

Lucie flipped the picture. "Anyway, this is where we're having breakfast. Croissants, baguettes, you know the thing." She laughed. "Not really. Then up here—"

Edee stopped listening. She pushed her covers back and stumbled to the window, pulling the shutters open and pressing her face against the glass. Almost immediately a person walked by carrying a baby. The person was covered. The baby was not. Edee stared as a realisation hit her. It was the same here and in France, and Dad had been covered too. This wasn't a one-off thing, a local thing. It was international. Global.

9

Twenty minutes later, the phone call had ended but she still hadn't moved. If it was international, then how could it be personal too? Except it had to be personal because she was the one with the glasses and without lines. Yet it was impossible to deny this new enormity and—*better*—something to finally go on. She still had no idea how she could possibly be similar to babies but, that aside, there was this thing. This obvious, glaring fact that no babies or toddlers—none she had seen—were covered by a barcode. Which meant that . . . somehow it came later.

Was something, *someone*, parcelling babies up inside a glittering wrapping?

She shivered.

Hang on. Was she somehow supposed to stop them from getting covered? Had she somehow ended up in the middle of some kind of weird sci-fi? Via an optician's? *Really*? And even if she had, what was she supposed to do with this . . . clue? She only knew one baby. Was she meant to follow Amber around until she got lines? Or tell Craig to be vigilant for something he couldn't even see? The man had looked in no state to hear such a thing. Tell Scotty? No.

Besides, it would be a terrible kind of sci-fi. She didn't know which side she was supposed to be on. Was it better to have the lines or not?

Another shiver goose-bumped her skin. The image she'd had in the optician's, the one of wrapped-up individual servings of meat in a chiller cabinet, came back into her head. The lines, the encasement. How *could* it be good?

But then, how had she managed to avoid whatever it was? Could some people have an in-built immunity? The way some people did with chicken pox or flu.

Immunity against what?

She pressed her face against the glass again, the frames clonking against the window, and watched one, two, three more uncovered infants going by.

Somehow, she stumbled through breakfast and then told Mum she was going to spend the morning on homework. As soon as she got back to her room, she grabbed her phone and scrolled back through the pictures until the beginning of photo time. There was no doubt. Over everybody else, the lines had always been there.

JUST AFTER LUNCH, Maddie text. *Me and Cass are going to town. Come too? Got something to show you!!*

Edee's first reaction was no. Not right now. But, then again, there would be more people in town. More babies. And she wasn't going to figure anything out by staying in her room all day. Throwing a few things into a bag, she headed into the hall and came to a stop just before Mum's office. "I'm going into town."

There was the rattle of the office chair over the floorboards and Mum rolled into the doorway. "Okay. Are you meeting anyone?"

She almost said no, because counselling and just *because*, but she didn't need the complication. "Cass and Maddie."

"Do you want a lift?" said Mum.

Edee was already turning away. "No."

Today, instead of the commuters, the park was full of lads running after a ball, another group lobbing a mini rugby ball back and forth, people walking, and families. Despite the surface differences, the place looked just as shiny and glittery. And from what she could see, the hypothesis—uncovered babies—was holding.

She stopped as the path forked. If she went straight across, town was a five-minute walk. If she went to the right it was longer but she'd go past the play area. She turned right.

A few minutes later, she stopped at a bench and pulled her phone from her pocket as if she were waiting for someone. She looked out over the top of it. The place had barely changed since she and Lucie used to come here, yet she hardly noticed that. She was too busy concentrating on the children. There were probably fifteen in all. The tiny ones were over the other side, the bigger ones were in front of her, and it was as obvious as it could be. The young ones were unlined. The older ones and the adults were covered.

She leaned forward. It struck her how strange it was that this whole scene was not interesting for the differences between the babies and everyone else, nor for the shining itself, but for the difference *between* the barcodes. Not only were the lines themselves different, but the quantity was different too.

The children nearest to her, the ones who had the lines, definitely had fewer than the adults. But some of the kids had more than the others. If she wanted to, if she didn't care about the crazy, she could've lined them up from least lined to most. Yet it wouldn't have gone by the size of the children or, therefore, by age. There was a boy on the tyre swing whose lines she could probably count from here, a girl at the top of the slide had more, and another girl on the climbing frame was somewhere in the middle.

Her eyes flowed from one to the next to the next.

The shining, when she wasn't so preoccupied by *weird* or *different*, was actually quite beautiful. The people looked a little like animated prisms except the light was less colourful.

But . . . wait . . . the girl on the climbing frame . . . her lines had disappeared. They'd vanished, as if they'd never been. Edee raised a hand to her face. The glasses were still there and everyone else was still shining.

What on earth?

With only a vague awareness of what she was doing, she stood and moved a step closer. And a second, and a third, and . . . the lines flickered back, as if someone, somewhere, had flicked a switch.

Stopping for a second to look up and around, as if there really might be some kind of button suspended in the sky, Edee then took another step towards the girl. She was staring. She knew she was, but it was impossible not to. The girl seemed oblivious. Seriously, how had that just happened?

"Can I help you?" said someone.

Her head turned towards the words but her eyes did not want to leave the girl, who was at the top of the climbing frame now.

"That's my daughter," said the same voice. "Who are you? What are you—"

The speaker was a couple of steps away. A woman. She did not look happy.

"Nothing," said Edee. "I, um, thought she was . . .

someone else. Sorry. I was . . . wrong." She turned, head down, heartbeat thundering, and rushed back to the path.

MADDIE WAS BEAMING. She had her phone in her hand. Cass was by her side, laughing. As Edee approached, she saw both of their faces change behind their shimmering lines.

"What's wrong?" said Maddie.

"What's happened?" said Cass at the same time. "You look like you're about to faint."

"Or spew." Maddie screwed up her face. "Please don't spew."

"Edes?" said Cass.

"I, um," said Edee. "Yeah, I . . . um." She couldn't say. She *couldn't*. But the two of them were looking at her like they'd just seen the barcodes for the first time. She had to say something.

"Something bad?" said Cass.

"I just saw . . . Lucie," said Edee, grabbing at the first thing she thought of. "I mean I thought I saw her. It was—"

"Aww," said Maddie. She screwed her face up in a different way, like Edee had transformed into a fluffy kitten. "That's so sweet."

Cass's eyebrows, however, were moving in the opposite direction. "You must be missing her if you're seeing things."

"It was . . . someone who looked like her," improvised Edee, the sentence trailing off. Her throat was dry.

"I don't think I've ever seen someone who looks like Lucie," said Cass.

"Yeah, we have," said Maddie.

"I wish we could go and visit her," said Cass.

"If we could stay in a hotel," said Maddie.

"I'd sleep on the camper van floor," said Cass. "Or in a

tent outside." She gave a sort of hopeful sigh. "In three years we can do what we want. If Lucie's still travelling then, I'm going to go and join her."

Maddie nudged her arm and made an unsubtle glance at Edee. "She'll be back by then. It's only a year."

Cass shrugged. "Yeah, I know. But just in case. Anyway, Lucie'll travel when she's eighteen, for sure, and I'm going too."

Edee adjusted the glasses.

Cass held her hand out. "Let's try them again."

Slowly, Edee took them off and handed them over. She squinted at the dullness.

Cass put them on, once more without a flicker of anything unusual, and looked at herself between the mannequins in the window behind them. "Isn't travelling supposed to be a bug? I reckon I've caught it. I feel like all I want to do is pack a bag and go somewhere. I don't even care where, just somewhere different. It's like my body's being pulled towards the airport, like the place is one ginormous magnet. Don't you ever feel like that?"

"Only to places that have swimming pools and hotels," said Maddie. "Maybe you just need a holiday?"

"No," said Cass. "A holiday would make it worse. I'd want to stay. I know I would." She hooked the glasses down her nose then pushed them back up with her index finger. "You know, someone, right now, is getting on a plane and off on an adventure. They have no idea what's going to happen. They might meet Lucie."

Edee curled her fingers inside her sleeves.

"We should plan something." Cass turned away from the window. Her face was glowing. "A proper trip when we're eighteen. How amazing would that be?"

"Yeah," said Maddie. "I guess. But it's ages away." She

pulled her phone from her pocket. "And this happened. Look."

She turned the screen towards them. Cass lifted the glasses up with a finger. She laughed. "That's awesome."

It was the photo of Lucie, Rosa, and Greg grinning at the mountainside cafe. However, now there were three additional faces peering down at them from the cafe's roof. It was well done. Funny. Edee looked away.

Maddie laughed. "I know, right. It took ages. I couldn't wait to see you see it. Shall we send it?"

"No," said Cass. "Let's do a call tonight so we can see her face when she sees it too. It'll be epic." She dropped the glasses to her nose again. "But not as epic as a trip."

"Come on," said Maddie, grabbing her arm and spinning her towards the door, "I need some epic jeans."

"I need a savings plan," said Cass. "And I'm going to get a job. We all should. Think how much we could save in three years. We'd have—"

Edee trailed behind the two of them. Her whole being was writhing with the possibility that epic had already happened today. Twice. The babies. The girl. It had to be epic . . . even if they all seemed oblivious and Edee had no clue what any of it meant.

10

"I got these," said Maddie, holding up a pair of jeans and turning them one way then the other to the camera. "And this." She held up a bag. It was so Maddie. One side had a diagonal strip of faux leopard print. "Aren't you missing shopping? Can you get stuff delivered?"

"We could," said Lucie. She was propped up on her narrow camper van bed. "But I haven't thought about it much." She raised her knee to the camera and pinched the thin, colourful fabric. "I got these in a market the other day. But I'm either wearing shorts or these and t-shirts. It's boiling."

"Yeah, we know." Cass made an overdone deadpan face. "No need to go on about it."

Lucie grinned. "I get it now. The less we spend, the longer we can do this. I'm totally fine wearing my stuff until it has holes."

Maddie screwed up her nose.

"Mum showed me the spreadsheet," said Lucie. "And,

anyway, I haven't missed anything yet. We've been too busy."

Edee was sitting on the floor, knees bent, leaning back against the wall in her room. *Anything*, or just stuff? She glanced at the jumper she was wearing and then to the box beside her wardrobe. Lucie-from-the-summer, old-Lucie, hadn't been able to bear getting rid of any of it.

"I'm going to get a job," said Cass. "Couldn't you get one too? There must be loads at the campsites."

"Probably," said Lucie. "I'll have to wait until we stay at one for more than a couple of days."

"Hey," said Maddie, looking away from the camera. "Check this out. I'm sending you something."

There was a pause, then Lucie laughed in such a Lucie-like way that it actually hurt. "That's the best thing ever. Did you do it, Mads?"

"Yeah," said Maddie. "I can't believe we had the perfect photo of us. It was the one from yours when—"

Edee silently recited the things she knew. The lines covered most people; they shone and they changed; some people seemed to be more covered than others; babies weren't covered at all; little kids didn't have as many lines; the lines could disappear.

"Hey, Edes."

"Huh?"

It was Lucie. "What's up?"

"Nothing," said Edee.

"Yes there is. That's the second time you've spaced out today."

"No," said Edee. She hadn't realised Lucie had noticed anything that morning. "I'm not. I just . . ."

"She's missing you," said Cass. "She thought she saw you earlier. She was full-on spooked."

Lucie's face softened. "I know. I'm missing you too. All of you."

"It's not the same," murmured Edee. "For you."

"Yeah, it is," said Lucie. "You're all there. Everything's different."

Edee said nothing.

"It's just"—Lucie shrugged—"you've got to choose to like it. Dad's right. There's no point being sad. It's a waste."

Except it hadn't been that simple when they'd been packing up her stuff. Edee couldn't help but notice Lucie's lines were glittering.

"I think it's nice," said Maddie, swivelling side to side on the chair in her room. The leopard print bag was still on her lap. "Missing people. It shows you care."

"It's like a movie," said Cass. "Best friends separated and a camper van getting further and further away." She grinned and leaned towards the camera. "That's why we should start planning something for all of us. A trip when we're eighteen. It'd be legendary. Luce, that's why I'm getting a job."

"Amazing!" said Lucie. "I am so up for that."

She was wrong, thought Edee. Lucie was never wrong. But on this she was. You couldn't simply choose to be okay with things. It wasn't possible. It would be like accepting the lines and not trying to find out what they were.

Cass was laughing. "Say that again."

"*Pamplemousse*," said Lucie. "I don't even like grapefruit but now I do just so I can say it. And *myrtilles*. How much better does that sound than blueberries?"

"Way better," said Cass.

"Oh, wait," said Lucie. "You'll love this one, *dépaysement*. It means . . . what was it? Oh, yeah. The feeling of being in a different place."

"Oh my God." Cass looked as if someone had promised

to whisk her off to the camper van right then. "That's what I want. How d'you say it again? Depay-what?"

The call finally ended half an hour later. Edee stared at the blank screen and tried to ignore the latest unsettled feeling that was occupying her belly.

The screen lit up again. Lucie was calling back.

She held the thing in her hand like it was an explosive.

The unsettled feeling turned into something more uncomfortable. She had never deliberately missed a call from Lucie before.

Seconds after the screen darkened, a message popped up. *Edes is it really just missing me? Is there anything else? I think there's something else??? xxx*

Her eyebrows pulled together a fraction. Just? No. It wasn't *just* anything.

She dropped the phone to the rug. Two weeks ago, they'd known everything about each other. Two weeks ago, Lucie would've been the first person she'd have told about random lines and Mum sending her to counselling. She hadn't told her about either of those things. And she didn't want to. No, she did. But not yet.

The screen illuminated again. No, wait, it was too fast. She couldn't not reply but she hadn't figured out what to say. She hadn't—

It wasn't Lucie.

It was a number she didn't recognise. Except she did. She'd seen it yesterday.

Hey, it's Scotty. Dad gave me your number so I could hijack another part of your weekend. Conspiracy?

If now had been some other time, she might have smiled, because he thought it was odd too. But now was now and she did not need Mum creating friends for her. Plus she had a message from her oldest friend and one from someone she barely knew. It should not be easier to know what to say to Scotty. The uncomfortable feeling in her belly twisted.

She typed fast—*Mum gave me yours too. Conspiracy for sure*—before switching—*Yeah, just missing you.* And then, only because there was too much going on, she added, *Happy you're loving it.* She threw the thing back on to the rug and headed out the door. It was only as she entered the lounge that she remembered she did not want to be there either. Because Mum. And counselling.

11

The unsettled feeling grew and grew that weekend. Edee would be doing some ordinary thing—walking, eating, watching the lines glitter around someone—and the counselling would wheedle its way into her mind, then her stomach would churn and churn and she'd try to come up with a way to avoid it (pretend to be sick, *be* sick, get lost on the way, say she'd forgotten about it).

Whenever Edee ventured out of her room, Mum kept saying how nice Maggie-the-counsellor was and what a great reputation she had. Each time, Edee did not say anything and, rather than taking the hint, Mum launched into a story about how Janice from work had gone to see her after having insomnia for two years, or how Janice's niece had gone about some phobia, or how Carmen had seen her about depression. At dinner, she went on to say how lucky they were she happened to have a cancellation right when they needed it.

Edee almost said it depended on your definition of lucky. And need.

She also almost reminded Mum that Carmen had

recommended the optician's and to look at how that had turned out. Except obviously she didn't. By the time they'd finished eating, it was almost impossible not to blurt out that if Mum liked Maggie-the-counsellor so much, then maybe she could go and talk to her instead. But she kept swallowing the words for the simple reason that she did not, right now, need the fallout. Besides, it turned out Mum was chaperoning her to the place. Every get-out clause was covered.

Monday was no better. The hours dragged and all Edee could think about was how she did not want to talk about Lucie or tell the counsellor about the lines (she'd rather talk about Lucie than that). Perhaps she could just not talk for the hour. No one could make her. It was a flimsy idea, too flimsy to be considered any kind of strategy, but it was an option and it lodged in her brain.

All in all, by the time she and Mum were sitting in the waiting room, Edee felt exhausted. Even the lines had seemed less interesting all day. Less anything. She'd shoved the glasses in her bag at the end of school because another headache was lurking and that was the last thing she needed. Well, no. The last thing was a counselling appointment. The headache came a close second.

"Hello. You must be Edee." The woman who had just emerged from the door opposite was holding out her hand.

Mum nudged Edee's elbow as she got up and Edee found herself standing and taking the hand (shaking hands? Already weird). If only the lines could somehow transform into some kind of alien space ship and whisk the counsellor off to some far-off planet.

"I'm Maggie," said the woman. She clasped Mum's hand next, then moved towards the receptionist's desk. "All the paperwork's up together?"

The receptionist nodded at the same time the phone rang. She turned to answer it.

"And we ran through everything the other day," said Maggie to Mum. "Confidentiality etcetera."

"Yes," said Mum.

Etcetera? What kind of person said etcetera?

Maggie turned towards Edee. "I like to speak to clients one to one but if you'd feel more comfortable, your mum is welcome to come in as well."

Comfortable? What part of this was supposed to be comfortable?

"And I'm flexible," said Maggie. "It can change from session to session."

"Edee?" said Mum.

"No, it's fine," muttered Edee.

Mum sat down again. "I'll be here if you need anything."

"Come through." Maggie headed back towards the door she'd emerged from and held it open. "There you are. Have a seat."

The space reminded Edee of a doctor's room, which was odd because there was nothing medical about it. She trudged towards the nearest chair. There were three in all, each a muted grey. They were separated by a circular rug with a flattened pile. To the side there was a low table. The walls held shelves that were dotted with bits and pieces. It was probably supposed to look inviting. It looked like a lounge that had gone wrong. She dropped her bag and sat down.

"Now," said Maggie, "before we get started, I want to repeat that everything we talk about is between us. The only time I will disclose anything is if I have concerns for your safety. You went through that with Ruby when your mum signed the forms?"

Edee nodded. Ruby the receptionist.

"So, it's lovely to meet you," said Maggie, with a smile that was probably supposed to be reassuring. "Today we'll get to know each other a little better. There's no commitment. If you don't think we are a good fit afterwards, then that's okay. Do you have any questions?"

Edee had looked away while the woman had spoken, her eyes coming to rest on the low table. It held a potted plant and a clock that was angled towards the counsellor. It also held a box of tissues. The top one was poking out. She stared the thing down. Mum might be able to decide she had to come here, but whatever else happened in this place there was no way she was going to cry. What a cliché. She shook her head.

"I understand you haven't spoken to a counsellor before," said Maggie. "Is that right?"

Edee nodded.

"And have you chosen to be here?"

Not speaking was all very well in theory, but it wasn't exactly practical when there were only the two of you in the room and the other person kept firing questions your way. Perhaps she'd try as few words as possible instead. She looked up. "No."

"Okay," said Maggie. "Like I said, there's no obligation. But I would like to get to know you a little better. Why don't you tell me about yourself? What do you like to do?"

Edee moved her gaze to the rug. She liked to be normal.

"If you weren't here," said Maggie, "what would you be doing?"

"Getting home from school," said Edee.

"Do you like school?" said Maggie.

Edee shrugged. "Yeah." When I'm not under surveillance.

"Are there any subjects you particularly like?"

There were lots of similar questions. Then Maggie went on to tell her how she'd become a counsellor and what she liked about her job. Edee started counting the objects in the room. There were three chairs, one rug, two potted plants, a row of seven glass ornaments on the window sill, another row of ten or eleven books on a shelf to the right of Maggie's head. The titles shouting things like 'feelings', 'emotions'—

"Now, I understand some things have changed recently," said Maggie, her tone shifting enough to interrupt the counting. "Your best friend has moved away."

"She's travelling with her family," said Edee.

"And you've been friends for a long time?"

"Yes." Mum would've told her this already. "Since we were two."

"So it's quite a big change?"

"Yes."

"I see. It must be difficult not seeing her every day?"

Is it really just missing me? Edee hesitated. Then nodded.

"What's her name?" Maggie spoke softly, like Edee might break when she said it.

"Lucie."

Maggie was quiet for a few moments. Her hands were clasped in her lap. No one sat like that in normal life. "We had something similar happen in our family," she said, eventually. "Although it was a bit different. Remember when I said that I changed jobs to this?"

Edee nodded again.

"Well, it coincided with us moving away for a while. My children were twelve and ten at the time. Would you like to hear about it?"

And not have to talk. Yes. She nodded once more.

"I'm not saying it's the same," said Maggie. "Everyone is different, of course, but we—"

Edee kept looking in the counsellor's rough direction while she let her mind wander (they can't know what we're thinking about). The shelf above her head was lined with cards. The pictures were mostly of the countryside or flowers, but one or two had 'thank you' in type that was readable from across the room. Maybe it was supposed to make you feel hopeful.

Or not. Janice, Janice's niece, and Carmen would've all sat here. People traipsing in, one after the other, with their problems. What a weird job. Maybe Craig should be here. All that shining he was covered by. The intense, thick stripes.

Wait. Was that it? The lines glowed the more stuff you had going on? And that's why they looked different? And babies weren't covered because they didn't have stuff going on yet. And that girl, the one on the climbing frame, she'd . . . well, maybe the lines absorbed the stuff that was going on like an emotion buffer sort of thing. And hers had finished absorbing all the stuff and had stopped glowing until something else came along. It sort of fitted. It was more plausible than a monster.

And . . . if that was the case, then surely a counsellor would have pale lines because dealing with stuff was their thing.

Edee nodded, like whatever Maggie was saying was super-interesting, and slipped her hand into her bag. Luckily, the glasses case was still at the top. She flipped it open and took them out one-handed, pulled the arms apart, and slipped them on.

The room seemed brighter.

But . . .

The woman looked just like everyone else. There was nothing different about her lines. In fact, other than a slightly different pattern, it could've been Mum's barcode or any of the other people she'd seen over the last few days.

Maybe she wasn't very good at counselling.

But all those people Mum had talked about seemed to think she was, and all those thank-you cards. So that was . . . interesting? Confusing?

She stretched her legs out in front, suddenly wanting nothing more than to move. Her feet were pricking with the start of pins and needles.

Whoa. She blinked. Once. Twice.

Her own legs were covered in lines.

Her body was.

What?

Glittering. Her whole body was glittering.

"Edee?" said Maggie. The woman might have been in another room or underwater.

She tried to pull her face straight, back to normal. Back to anything like normal. Her heart was thundering. She glanced at her arm to double, triple-check, but she didn't need to. Light was radiating from her. *From her.* How? When? There'd been nothing at school. There'd been nothing when she'd got into Mum's car and taken the glasses off.

"That seemed to resonate," said Maggie. "Could you tell me why? What crossed your mind then?"

"Um," said Edee. She had *lines.* Her body was shining. Glittering. Exactly like everyone else's, which was . . .

Maggie leaned back. Her hands were folded in her lap now. Her own lines were glittering a little more. The room seemed twice as bright. It *was* twice as bright. Edee scanned from one side to the other and back again. The monster . . . what if that was right after all? What if something had been in here and covered her with this? But the place was empty.

67

Or, rather, empty of anything other than plants and books and ornaments and things. There were no—

"Edee?" said Maggie again.

"I, um, no," managed Edee. She was squinting. "I just . . . the glasses are new. I was getting a headache."

The counsellor nodded slowly and glanced at the clock. "Well perhaps we should leave it there for today. What do you think?"

Edee nodded.

"It can take a while to get to know each other," said Maggie. "That's perfectly normal." She paused. "I'd suggest you reflect on this session over the coming days, and if you'd like to come back let Ruby or your mum know and we can book something in."

Edee's throat was dry, raspy. She coughed. "Okay."

"This has been a little shorter than normal," said Maggie. "We could do one more with no further commitment if that would help you make up your mind. Have a think about it." She held out a card. "Those are my contact details. If anything comes up or you have any questions, you're welcome to get in touch with me. Your mum has a copy too."

Edee nodded again, watching her own glittering hand as she took it. What if she had lines in this room but nowhere else?

"I enjoyed meeting you," said Maggie, standing up. "And if we get the chance to meet again, that would be lovely." She paused again then smiled. "We all go through ups and downs. In my experience, talking about it is usually a weight off our minds. Even if it seems difficult at first." She opened the door and held out a hand. Edee walked past.

Glittering Mum looked up and from Edee to Maggie. "That went fast. Everything alright?"

"Yes," said Maggie. "Edee's going to have a think about

everything and let you know if she'd like another appointment."

Mum looked from one to the other again and gave a slow nod. She opened her mouth and shut it again.

In the background, Ruby the receptionist was glittering too.

"I do," Edee blurted out. If she only had lines here then . . . she had to. "I mean one more. I've got a headache. I couldn't concentrate."

Mum looked relieved. She slipped her laptop into its sleeve and stood quickly. "Let's get it booked in then."

Maggie's mouth moved into a smile, but her face was unreadable. It was the kind of look Edee had failed at a few moments ago. "Of course. There's a regular slot available on Tuesday at the same time, or book another one-off for Monday, whichever you prefer."

"We'll take the Tuesday," said Mum, moving towards the reception desk.

Edee stared down at her shining, glittering body. She could feel the counsellor looking at her but, right then, she did not care.

12

"You look tired," said Mum, as they walked back to the car.

Edee bit her lip. She did not look tired. She looked shiny. The glittering had not disappeared in the reception area nor when they'd left the building. Right now, she was watching her vertically lined legs and feet as they moved across the pavement.

"Is it just a headache?"

Just. No. "Yeah. I . . . it was intense."

"She's nice though, isn't she," said Mum. This time it wasn't a question.

Edee nodded. She could not manage anything else.

"Although I'd love to get my hands on the place," said Mum. "A few tweaks to the colour palette would make such a difference. Maybe I'll suggest it when we get to know her a little better."

"Mmm," muttered Edee. She could feel Mum looking at her. "I mean, yeah. It was grey." Grey? Even for her it was lame. But she was *glittering*. She rubbed the sides of her head like it really was painful. It *was* painful. Painful from trying to figure this out, because how could she have gone from nothing to full-on glittering in less than an hour? And, more than that, she'd hardly taken the glasses off in the last forty-eight hours. Why had she had to at the exact point that had happened? Or had the lines arrived because she'd taken them off? Or was it a case of the worst timing ever?

Mum nudged her arm. She was holding out a half-used strip of painkillers. "I was hoping we could go out for a bite to eat. Why don't you take one of these and we'll see how it is when we get back to the car? If you don't feel up to it, we can go straight home."

Once more Edee found herself going along with it. She popped one of the tablets out and pulled her water bottle from her bag. All the while, she watched her hands glitter.

———

MUM CHOSE the Italian that was five minutes from home. She'd said Edee could choose but that was not happening; Edee would've been hard pressed to choose a chocolate from a selection box right then. As it was, she'd picked the first pizza her eyes had fallen on and then nipped to the bathroom.

She'd stood staring at the mirror for ages like she was appraising some kind of unfathomable picture in a gallery. By the time she'd got back, Mum had ordered. She'd now headed to the bathroom and Edee was back to staring at her hands. She ran one set of fingers across the skin on the back of the other one. It felt exactly as if she was running her fingers over the back of her hand. No more, no less. She closed her eyes and repeated the movement. There was nothing; no hint that anything else was in between. Opening them again, she raised the hand up, brought it level with her face, then moved it side to side. It was impossible to see if there was a gap between the lines and her skin. But there must be because the lines couldn't be inside the skin. It wasn't as if the skin itself was glowing. And, whoa, of course, the lines were over the top of her clothes. She pulled her sleeve up, but the lines sort of fluidly went from covering her jumper to covering her arm. They had to be separate. Yet she pinched the skin and it moved in perfect symmetry with the lines.

"Edee?"

She let go and tried to look like pinching your own skin was a reasonable thing to be doing in a restaurant. A frown was lining Mum's forehead. Her eyes were preoccupied.

"Um . . . everything's so clear," said Edee. She tried to come up with something else but she couldn't. The truth was easier. And crazier. "My skin . . . looks different with the glasses on."

Mum slipped into her seat. Her lips moved a little like a question was hovering on them.

With, for once, impeccable timing, Edee's phone lit up. She grabbed it as her brain simultaneously registered that, in comparison to her hand, the screen looked *dull*.

It was Scotty: *I just thought, what if it was a double conspiracy? How do you know I'm me on this number and you're you?*

"Who's that?" said Mum.

Edee turned the phone over and said, "Lucie," instantly regretting it. She should've said Cass or Maddie.

Mum straightened her knife and fork. "How's she finding everything? Difficult, I imagine."

It was clearly not the question she had been going to ask a few moments ago but Edee was simply relieved that the concerned look was, however temporarily, being directed at someone else. Yet still she could not make anything up. "She's loving it."

"Is she?" said Mum. "Well it's all new and exciting I

suppose." She pressed her forefinger and thumb down on the fork, rocking it side to side, and gave a tiny shake of her head. When she spoke again, her voice was low. "I still find it so hard to believe they've done this now. It's such an important year. I wish they'd thought it all through a bit more, for everyone's sake. It must be so unsettling for her, however she seems."

It was Edee's turn to frown. What part of 'she's loving it' had Mum not heard?

"I mean, there's going to be fallout for her. There has to be," said Mum, louder. She looked up. "Are you finding it difficult to hear she's enjoying it? Because it might not be true. Did you mention it to Maggie?"

And what part of confidential had she not heard?

"I know," said Mum, holding her hands up like Edee had just said that out loud. The lines on her hands were now at a slightly different angle to her body. "Your time with Maggie is for you only. It's just, I worry."

Her lines had notched up another level. It was like sitting opposite a laser light show. Edee squinted then looked away into the restaurant and into . . . paleness, faintness. Her eyes widened. She blinked.

"Have you been in contact with Scotty?" said Mum. "In some ways his world has been turned even further upside down."

The paleness belonged to the waitress who was heading to their table. Did her barcode look faint because Mum's was currently so bright? No. Compared to everyone else in here it was faint. She had lines and they were shining, but they were less what? Intense? Edee could not help herself. She leaned forward.

"Edee?" said Mum.

"The . . . food," she managed.

"Risotto?" said the waitress, smiling.

"That's me," said Mum. "Thank you."

"And Margherita?"

Edee nodded and clasped her hands in her lap to stop herself grabbing the arm that was centimetres away. How could it look like that? Why? For a moment she could do nothing but stare then, slowly, she lifted the glasses up. The waitress—she was probably only a couple of years older than Edee—looked ordinary. Completely ordinary.

"And there's a salad to come," said the waitress.

"Thank you. It looks lovely," said Mum. There was a touch of tightness in her voice now. "Are you sure you don't want something else to go with yours?"

Edee nodded.

"Olives?"

Edee shook her head.

"We can share the salad," said Mum.

The waitress moved away and Edee dropped the glasses back down. The faint lines returned. Was she in some sort of halfway stage that Edee had unknowingly gone through in the counselling room? Would she reach full glitter by the time the pizza was eaten? Or by the time she came back with the salad?

"Janice was telling me how few people get their five-a-day," said Mum, with forced brightness. "It was shocking. Less than a third. I was thinking we should start having smoothies for breakfast a few times a week. Apparently they can be mood lifting too."

The woman behind the bar and the two other waiting staff looked as glittering as everyone else. It couldn't have anything to do with this place.

"What do you think?" said Mum. "At the weekend when we have more time. We could make them together."

"Huh?" said Edee.

"Smoothies," said Mum, the space between her eyes

creasing again. "Would you like to make some on Saturday?"

"Uh," said Edee. "Yeah."

The waitress—still palely covered—reappeared. Moments later, she put the salad bowl down and gave another smile. "Would you like any Parmesan? Black pepper?"

"No, thank you," said Mum. "Edee?"

She shook her head. Beyond the faint lines, there was a name badge. *Kitty.*

"Enjoy your food," said Kitty. She touched Mum lightly on the arm. "That risotto is gorgeous by the way." She turned and headed towards another table.

Edee watched her every step.

"Someone you know?" said Mum.

"Huh?" said Edee.

Mum pinched some salad between the servers and set it down on her plate. The cutlery clunked against the china. "The waitress. Is she someone you know?"

"No." Edee's eyes magnetically drifted towards the paleness again. "I don't know. She looks, um, familiar."

"Really?" said Mum, twisting in her seat to look.

It was like a ghost barcode. Or as if someone had turned down a dimmer switch. But how? Why? Always, it was the same questions. Yet, other than the babies, this was the first person who'd looked different. Distinctly different. Edee stopped mid-chew. It was . . . as if a neon sign had unfurled from the ceiling. She needed to speak to her. Obviously she did.

"She can't be much older than you," said Mum, scooping up some of the rice. "Perhaps she went to school round here. Let's ask her."

Edee's heartbeat thudded. No. Yes. But not right now.

Not with Mum here. She wriggled a slice of pizza free. "No."

Everything around them seemed extra loud: the burbling voices, the clinking glasses, the laughter.

Mum put down her fork and clasped her hands above the plate, her elbows on the table. "Edee, I'm proud of you for going to the appointment today. I really am. It feels like a big step forward. And I know it's difficult, with Lucie moving and being the age you are. I understand. Truly I do. It is difficult when someone moves away, whatever the circumstances."

A piece of gooey cheese was hanging from the pizza slice. Edee focused on it. She could feel her heartbeat pulsing in her squirming stomach. Mum meant Dad. But it was not the same. Mum hadn't seen who-knew-what when Dad had gone back home.

"But you have to be open to meeting new people," said Mum. "There are so many out there and you might even get on with them better than Lucie. You won't know until you give them a chance. It doesn't mean you can't be friends with her too."

The piece of cheese blobbed to the plate. Edee squashed it with her finger. Not now. Not right now.

"Edee," said Mum.

She looked up. Mum was shining like a human glitter ball. "Cass wants us all to go travelling when we're eighteen."

"I'm sorry?" Mum rubbed her forehead. "Did you hear what I said?"

"Yes," said Edee. "And I don't want to talk about it."

Mum frowned. She opened her mouth as if to say something else. Then took another spoonful of risotto instead.

Edee looked away, towards Kitty.

13

I t was like she suddenly had a purpose. All evening and all Tuesday morning, Edee tried to come up with ways to talk to Kitty. Before getting back to the obvious— she was going to have to go back to the restaurant—she trawled the internet and, for the second time in a week found nothing. To be fair, a first name, a restaurant name, and a face wasn't much to go on. Maybe Kitty was short for something. Dashing to the toilet between lessons, she found a name website and then searched on various spellings of Katherine, as well as half a dozen less likely possibilities. Still there was nothing.

So . . . the restaurant. The thing was, it wasn't as if she had enough money to eat out every day or the freedom to be out every evening. Then again, one of the reasons Mum liked the place so much was because it transformed from daytime cafe to evening restaurant. More often than not, any time they went there, she spent half the time talking about the reason the transformation worked so well and how she would love to work on something similar.

But anyway, what if Kitty worked daytime shifts too?

Although Edee supposed she could hardly keep popping in on the off chance she was there or lurk at the window every day.

The whole thing was still occupying her brain as they headed to the canteen for lunch. Maybe she could drop in on the way home tonight. If she got the bus she'd have enough time. Maybe she could pretend she'd left something behind last night or maybe—

"Oh my God," said Maddie. Her face was directed towards the inside of her pocket. "Did you see Lucie's message?"

"No," said Cass.

Edee shook her head. They'd just had history. When she'd come out of the toilet, she'd buried her phone in the bottom of her bag.

"Rosa and Greg are making her go on a retreat," said Maddie. "No electricity, electronics or cooked food for three days. They are so going to join a cult one day."

"Why no cooked food?" said Cass.

"Seriously?" said Maddie. "She's going offline for three days with a bunch of weirdos and you're bothered about no hot food?"

"I suppose because it's so sunny." Cass was peering into the curved counter that held metal containers filled with chips and pasta. "That would make sense. And loads of people go on retreats. It's really normal."

"Do you think they're even allowed to talk?" said Maddie.

Cass laughed. "I hope so. Can you imagine Lucie on a silent retreat? Does she mind?"

Maddie had twisted towards Edee for extra cover and was typing one-handed. "I'm asking her."

"She'd have said if she did," said Edee. She felt strangely flat at the news. Maybe it was a good thing. Maybe she'd have stuff figured out in three days. Wait. A good thing? In what world could it possibly be a good thing to be out of contact with Lucie?

"True." Cass picked up a tray. "Hey, I forgot. Dad said the hairdressers by his office has an advert up for Saturday staff." She shivered. "But dead hair, it's—"

"All hair's dead," said Maddie.

"Yeah but dead unattached hair," said Cass, pulling a face. "Disgusting."

Edee's brain leapt in a way that seemed at odds with everything else going on inside it. Of course. How obvious. She could go into the cafe and ask about a job.

———

"You're a genius," said Cass, as they got off the bus and turned left. "If they only need one person then obviously you should have it, but imagine if they needed two. It would be amazing. And we could put a word in for Maddie. Once we've got jobs, she'll want one as well. Babysitting doesn't pay much."

Edee had tried to shake her off—how could she speak to Kitty about the lines with Cass there?—but given that she didn't know how she was going to talk about the lines anyway, maybe it was better to have someone else there. Plus Cass was at least interested in a job.

The nearer they got, the more Edee's heartbeat quickened. What if Kitty wasn't there? What if she was? What if she was covered by ordinary lines today and she'd missed her chance to find something out? What if she wasn't as friendly as she'd seemed and dismissed Edee like some little kid? Her hands found their way to the glasses, lifting and then settling them again.

Cass grabbed her arm, pulling it down and looping hers

through it. "I'm so excited. Doing this is telling the universe that travelling is going to happen. Do you think that stuff works? I do."

Edee gave a non-committal, "Mmm."

"I know you're missing Luce," said Cass. "We all are. But it's like her going away has kicked everything into perspective, you know? Like it's made everything clear. I know what I want. I mean, I wish I had her parents, but I can make it happen for myself some day."

"Great," managed Edee, with the one percent of focus not consumed by the door that was five steps away. Four. Three. Two.

Cass let go of her arm and pushed it open.

Edee scanned the place and anticipation stuttered into disappointment. No Kitty.

"Who should we ask?" said Cass. She was standing on tiptoes and craning one way then the other.

The daytime staff wore navy aprons. There was one at the counter and two others talking to customers.

"At the counter, I guess," said Edee. She looked left and right again just in case she'd been mistaken. She hadn't. Everyone in here was glittering away.

"Come on," said Cass. "Do you want to or shall I?"

"You," said Edee. "You're better at it." Maybe Kitty was in the kitchen.

The two of them wove between the tables. The area that last night had been the bar was now a coffee counter, as if it was a totally different place. Edee checked herself. It wasn't important. She wasn't Mum.

Cass put her hands on the counter. "Hello."

The waiter turned around. "Hello there."

"Sorry to interrupt."

He held up the tea towel and glass. "Be my guest."

Cass laughed.

"What can I get you?" he asked.

"Nothing at the moment, Ty," said Cass, with an unsubtle nod to his name badge. "Although we could help you with the glasses?"

The waiter smiled. "Observant and helpful. What's the catch? You're selling something?"

"No catch. I'm Cass. This is Edee. We're looking for jobs and we'd love to work here."

This was Cass in full flow. Her lines were glittering. So were his.

He was still smiling. "And I'd love to help. But you'll have to speak to Freddie. He's the owner. He's sorting out a delivery at the moment. You're welcome to wait."

Cass glanced at Edee, who nodded.

"How long have you worked here?" said Cass. She pulled out one of the stools.

Edee slipped round to her other side and onto the one nearest to the kitchen. There was a small window in the kitchen door. She could see a rack of ingredients, nothing more.

"A year," said Ty. "I started here when I started at college."

"The tech?" said Cass.

"Yeah."

"Did you go to Willmott's?" said Cass.

"Sure did."

"Thought so," said Cass. "I didn't recognise you. I can't wait for college."

"It's better than school," said Ty, picking up another glass. He lowered his voice. "And better than working."

"But you get paid here," said Cass.

"I do," said Ty.

Edee scanned the room once more. It did seem to be just the three members of staff at the moment. Would that be enough? Could Kitty be helping with the delivery?

"Do they give jobs to people who're at school?" said Cass.

Ty buffed the glass as he spoke. "Freddie's daughter works some Saturdays. She's sixteen, I think. Goes to St Luke's."

"I wish my parents owned a cafe," said Cass. "What should we say to him? Have you got any tips?"

Ty pushed his lips forward and tilted his head to the side. His hands stilled.

Cass leaned her forearms on the counter.

Some people would probably assume that being around her was not so different to being around Lucie. And, in some ways, that was true. In others, it was not at all. Had Lucie been here, for example, she would more than likely be chatting to him too, but that would've been because she'd have found it impossible not to. Talking was like breathing for her. Cass, however, was not like that. She'd started the conversation for a particular reason and she wouldn't give up until she'd got what she wanted. Edee shifted on the stool and let her eyes drift around the cafe once more, over the light that was coming from every direction.

"No way!" Cass leaned forward. Her arm nudged Edee's. "I cannot believe that."

"I can't believe you've never heard of it," said Ty. He was walking backwards towards a woman who had just arrived at the counter. He turned. "Hello there. What can I get you?"

The woman smoothed her hair. "Flat white. To go."

Cass was staring at him.

"Did you know that?" said Cass.

"No," said Edee, hoping that was the right answer.

"I am so glad we came here," said Cass. She leaned to the side and mouthed. "He's amazing."

Edee stared and stared again because a bead of light had just appeared at the top of Cass's head. In a nanosecond, it zoomed down over her front, round the back, and then joined up with itself again. The new line glowed. It *burned*.

Edee stopped breathing. Had Cass ignited?

The picture in front of her connected with the words in her brain and she lurched forward, swatting at her friend's back with her hand. Her *hand*. But the line was cool, yet still it shone as if it were alight.

"Oh Edes." For a split second, Cass looked confused, then she leaned in and pulled her into a sideways hug like this was ordinary; like Edee was the kind of person who went round dishing out random hugs. Hugs that involved slapping people on the back.

Their heads bumped together. Clumsy. Awkward. And all the while Edee stared at the strip of light that had appeared from nowhere and was still shining like a beacon around Cass's body.

"He's . . . look at him," muttered Cass into Edee's ear. She stayed a few more seconds before pulling back.

Edee did not look anywhere but at the line. She had just noticed something else. There was something within the skinny ring of sun that was circling her friend.

14

She leaned a little more forward. She had to because the whatever-it-was in the line was so minuscule that, even with the glasses on, it was hard to see. It was darker than the background light, but it was the light too. It, no, *they* were . . . symbols. A row of symbols that went all the way around.

"What are you doing?" said Cass, twisting to look over her shoulder.

Edee was near. Too near. Invading-personal-space near. "I . . . um . . . a bug." She swept her hand across Cass's back.

Her friend twisted the other way, trying to see. "Is it a money spider? Say it's a money spider. They're lucky."

"I don't know. It's gone," lied Edee. The line was still burning; the symbols still there. In a second or two she had scanned the beams above them, the floorboards below, and everything in-between. Once again nothing was out the ordinary. Nothing else had changed. The place was full of the same people. None of them had even moved. The bead had apparently appeared from nowhere. How was that even possible?

"You should've put it outside," whispered Cass. "People don't want spiders in their drink."

"Yeah . . . I guess." The harder she tried not to look at the beam of light circling Cass, the more her eyes felt magnetised towards it. "Are you feeling okay?"

"What?" said Cass, back to normal volume. "Yeah, great. Amazing." She paused and tilted her head. "I should be asking you. You look like you did the other day in the park."

Edee forced her pupils away from the shining to meet Cass's. It wasn't much of a movement. A millimetre, if that.

"You're not, right?" said Cass.

"What?"

"Thinking you're seeing Lucie again?" She looked over her shoulder.

"No," said Edee. Even though it was true, she knew it didn't sound convincing because there was that symbol thing. Just there. Radiating. Wait. She blinked once, then again. It was radiating but dimming. Moments ago, that strip had been a beacon of fire. Now it was getting harder and harder to distinguish it from all the others.

Cass's focus slipped past her. "He's coming back. Be normal, Edes."

Even in the midst of shining fiery symbols, it felt like a punch. *Be normal.*

"Got your head around it yet?" said Ty.

Edee's body contracted. He knew? How could he know?

"Wanderlust," said Cass, leaning forward on her elbow again. "We've got a friend who's travelling in France. She taught us this word the other day: *dépaysement*. Have you heard of it?"

Ty's lips turned downwards as he shook his head. He wasn't talking about the glowing beads and lines. Of course he wasn't.

"It's the feeling of being in a different place," said Cass. "French has an actual word for it. I thought that was good but wanderlust is so much better. It's me."

"Cass Wanderlust." Ty had moved into a casual leaning-back-on-the-counter pose, like he was in an advert. Like he *was* an advert. "You might not want to say it out loud too much."

She laughed.

"What about you?" said Ty.

Edee barely registered he was speaking to her. The symbols had disappeared, she was sure of it. But the line had not. It had just dulled a little.

"Edes," said Cass, nudging a foot against her leg. "It's her best friend who's moved away."

"You can't be shy if you want to work in a cafe," said Ty.

Shy? Who had said shy? No one. He'd—

"Come on. Cass is all about the wanderlust. What about you? I want facts."

Facts? She had tons of them. Or, if not facts, potential facts. That bead. The light. The lines. Symbols. And yet they were the wrong kind of facts and she could not think of a single other thing to say. A single thing she *wanted* to say to him or, right now, to Cass.

"If I'm going to put in a good word for you, I need something to go on," said Ty.

"You'd do that?" Cass leaned forward once again. She was looking at him like he'd promised her the world.

"Sure," said Ty.

Edee did not want him to put in a good word for her.

With terrible timing, her eyes tingled. Except it wasn't a tingling. It was a burning and it felt like the world was pressing down on her lungs at the same time. Only, not the world. It was an absence of the world. It was an awful, awful absence. It was missing Lucie times a thousand. Sliding from the stool she muttered something about going to the toilet. Neither of them seemed to hear.

The few steps from the stool to the door felt like a mile. In an unexpected piece of good fortune, the bathroom was empty. As soon as the door thudded shut, she let out a shaky sob. Standing by the side of the sink in front of the mirror with her hands trembling, she made herself take long, slow breaths. Cass had been next to her. She wasn't alone. Not really. But the absence was a grip, a tight, tight grip. She would not have been surprised to see fingers curled around her ribs.

She looked into the mirror. There were no fingers. Just lines. The same some-shining, some-dull lines. And, even in the midst of everything else, she was filled with the impossibility that Cass could have been unaware of that bead of light. On her own body. Except, it was all too believable. Utterly believable. She pulled the glasses a few centimetres down her nose and peered over the top. Because *that*. Nothing.

Had she been cursed? Was she destined to walk through life seeing this stuff unless she took the glasses off? But even then she couldn't forget because she knew.

Reaching a hand towards the mirror, she watched the real lines meet the reflected lines, then traced the outline of the frames in the glass. Her finger paused. Reflected-Edee had lines going over her eyes, just like everyone else. But her —flesh-Edee—could not see them. Looking out through the glasses she should be seeing vertical bars. In fact, through the brightness she shouldn't be seeing much at all, but her sight was uninterrupted. It was clear. In fact, with the lenses it was clearer than normal. Did that mean . . . what did that mean?

The heavy door to her left began creaking. Edee spun away from the mirror and shoved her hand under the dryer, blasting the space with noise. A tiny, tiny part of her panicked that this time she had unintentionally conjured up a thing. A thing connected to the lines that was entering this bathroom. A thing that made beads appear around people. Her heart thunked.

But it wasn't a thing. It was a person. And, even as she realised that, she managed to also think, please not Cass. Not yet.

It wasn't.

It was Kitty. Faint-lined Kitty.

"Hello there." Kitty was propping open the door with her foot and tugging a cleaning caddy behind her. "Did I make you jump? I'm sorry."

Edee shook her head and found herself saying, "Don't you wait tables?"

"I do," said Kitty, glancing over again. This time with recognition. "You were here last night. You ate a Margherita."

"Yes," said Edee. "How come you're cleaning today?"

"A bit of extra money," said Kitty. She set a spray bottle down by the sink. "And I like it."

"You like it?" said Edee. Cleaning?

Kitty pulled a cloth from the caddy and nodded. Her lines were glittering, like anyone else's would. But, just like last night, it was as if a dimmer switch had been dialled down.

"Yeah. People never believe me but it's true," she said, buffing a tap. "What brings you back here today?"

"I . . ." started Edee. "My friend wants a job. We thought there might be one here."

"It's a good place to work," said Kitty. She smiled. "I mean, this is my second week but so far it is."

"Are you at college?" said Edee. She might have been a bit older than that actually. "Uni?"

"No," said Kitty, buffing the final tap. "I was. I left."

"You left uni?" said Edee.

"Yeah." Kitty buffed the second to last tap.

People *left* uni? "Why?"

"Lots of reasons. Mostly because I wasn't enjoying it."

Be normal. She found Cass's words back in her head. Leaving uni wasn't normal, was it? "Are you in a band?"

Kitty glanced up. She looked amused. "No."

"A painter?"

"No," said Kitty. "Really, I wasn't enjoying it."

"What are you going to do?" said Edee.

"Instead of uni?" said Kitty.

"Yeah."

"I don't know," said Kitty. "This for now. See what happens."

"Don't you want to know?" Edee was trying to imagine telling her mum that. She couldn't. She wouldn't.

"No," said Kitty. She said it with such conviction. The faint lines glittered.

"Do you ever think you're different to other people?" The question was out of Edee's mouth before she considered it might sound rude; before she even knew she was going to say it.

"Different?" said Kitty. "How?"

"Just different," said Edee. "I mean . . . different."

Kitty picked up the bottle and sprayed the sink. She didn't seem to mind being asked. More, she seemed to be considering it. The faint lines shimmered. "No, not really."

But she was wrong. The evidence was right there, wrapped around her.

"Does it matter?" said Kitty.

"No," said Edee. "Yes. I mean . . . maybe."

Kitty smiled. "Interesting. Say more."

Had she thought about it, Edee would've been amazed her cheeks did not burn. But she didn't and they didn't. "I . . . it's, I don't know, sometimes I think people are more different than they realise. I wondered if anyone else thought that too."

Kitty swirled the cloth back and forth a few times. "What if it's the opposite?"

The opposite? The opposite of different? But that didn't make sense. Kitty was different.

For a few seconds, the sound of the cloth swishing was all there was. Then the door to the left creaked again and the doorway filled with Cass. "There you are. Freddie's free."

Here it was, thought Edee. The evidence. Light to the left, faintness to the right. Opposite. Different.

Cass glanced at Kitty. Edee wished she had stayed chatting to Ty.

"Hello," said Kitty. "You're after a job here?"

"Yeah," said Cass. "Hopefully. Come on, Edes. He hasn't got much time."

Edee did not want to come on, but Cass was looking all expectant and hurried and now someone else was behind her waiting to come into the toilet.

"Good luck," said Kitty. "Although you won't need luck. He's really nice."

Cass smiled.

"Thanks," said Edee. She moved slowly towards the door.

It was so weird. Nothing had happened—if anything she felt more confused—yet, even though none of this line business made sense, she was suddenly filled with a peculiar certainty that somehow it did.

15

The certainty stayed with her through the short meeting with Freddie. (He took their details in case anything came up, and told them he'd need to apply for a permit because they were at school). It seemed to buoy her through the walk home while Cass went on and on about Ty and how he'd given her his number—"Edes, he's seventeen. He has a car." It stayed through a text chat with Lucie, who was packing for the retreat, and it even accompanied her up to the front door of the apartment and into the kitchen to make a drink.

And then she caught a glimpse of herself in the hallway mirror.

Lines, lines, lines.

Lines like an ordinary person.

And unlike Kitty.

Kitty who thought everyone was the same, even when it was obviously not true. Kitty who hadn't minded her asking about different. Kitty who had left uni and was totally fine about it. A person, Edee was sure, who knew something about the lines.

If only she could be like her.

Who was she kidding? She could never be like Kitty.

Obviously she couldn't.

Because she was Edee. Edee who sometimes—often—didn't know what to say. Like today with Ty. Kitty would've known what to say to him. Of course she would. She probably did. Daily, on their shifts together. And if she didn't, she wouldn't have minded. No, actually, she'd have been so interesting he would never have asked that question of her in the first place.

And if Kitty's best friend had moved away, she'd probably float through the whole experience like a helium balloon. She'd probably *be* the one moving away. Maybe she had. Maybe somewhere there was another version of Edee whose life had changed without her asking it to. But, anyway, whatever the circumstances, Kitty had faint—*interesting*—lines, and Edee did not.

It took her a moment or two to notice the bead. Perhaps it became too bright not to notice. Perhaps it was a chance look up. Perhaps it was something else entirely. Whatever the reason, her eyes fixed on the reflected blob above her head an instant before it began to zoom. Her chin snapped down, slow in comparison, and she watched the bead reach her feet, disappear for a nanosecond, then zip back up her calves. She twisted just in time to see it race up her back in the mirror, rejoin itself, and glow. Exactly like it had on Cass. And—she leaned so far forward her forehead bumped into the glass—like Cass's, there were symbols. Except . . . they weren't symbols. They were letters.

Letters in a string. A backwards string.

She took a shaky step back from the mirror, bent forward, and strained her neck trying to read sideways:

ossibletobedifferentimpossibletobedifferentimpossibletobedifferentimpossib

Her eyes watered from the effort of trying to read the tiny, tiny letters from this awkward orientation. How could there be letters circling her? Where had they come from? Why?

Wait. Her head moved so fast, her neck cricked. Up, down, left, right. But there was nothing, no one in here.

She stared downwards again and blinked a couple of times, her vision blurring. Her hands went to the glasses. Don't fail now. Please. But it wasn't the glasses. It was the letters. They were running into each other like a line of ink that had been splattered with water and, as she watched, they became unreadable, melting into the background before the whole thing glowed. It could've been any one of the other ton of lines that were glowing right now.

Scalding tea slopped down her hand, ripping her awareness back to the hallway and back to her skin. Her flesh was searing. It seemed too ordinary to go to the kitchen and run the cold tap, but that's what she did. The cool water cascaded over her hand for a minute, two. Then, with terrible timing, the front door clicked. Edee closed her eyes and tried to pull every piece of herself together. She turned the tap off and wiped her hands.

Moments later Mum came through the door. "There you are. Good day?"

"Yeah." The word was out of Edee's mouth before the total absurdity of it registered.

"Get back late?" said Mum, nodding towards her uniform.

"Yeah." She cupped her cold hands around the cooling mug. Once more the truth—a part of the truth—was all she could manage. "Cass wants a job. I went with her to ask about one."

"A job?" said Mum. "What kind of job? Where?"

"It was a cafe, although I don't think she minds that

much," said Edee. It was so bizarre to be having this conversation right now. Her eyes kept straying to the lines over her body. "She just wants to earn some money."

"What about school?" said Mum.

"On Saturdays," said Edee.

"Are her parents okay about that?" said Mum. "Do they know?"

"I don't know," said Edee. "Probably."

Mum's lines were—predictably—glittering. Edee wondered about the letters that would have once glowed along them, and whether they only appeared once, and whether the lines ever disappeared.

Wait. Cass's line had been full of symbols, not letters.

Mum headed towards the fridge and touched her on the arm as she passed. The two sets of lines butted up against each other. "I'd rather up your allowance than have you being distracted by a job."

Edee busied herself with a sip of cooling tea, hoping the mug would cover enough of her face to hide the expression she knew was on there. The one that would betray the fact she was more distracted, more confused, than she'd ever been in her whole life. She edged towards the door. "I'm going to get changed and, um, do some homework." Without lingering on the lie or waiting to hear the reply, she turned and rushed along the hallway. Once there, she closed the door and stood in front of the round mirror that hung above the chest of drawers. Her fingers brushed her face, trying to find the line. Was it that one or that one or that one? It was impossible to know. It could've been any of them.

The thing had sprouted from her own head, like a peculiar looping strand of luminous hair. It was hard to know if she felt sick or wonder or something else entirely. How could she have been so sure it all made sense an hour ago? The thing had grown from her own head.

Sick. She felt sick. And she wanted to talk to Lucie. Right now. She didn't care about any of the other stuff. The timing, the being okay stuff. That thing had popped out of her own head. And Cass's. She needed to tell someone. She needed to tell *Lucie*. And, when she had, Lucie would understand the spaced out thing. She would be on her side. She would help her out.

Edee grabbed her phone from her pocket.

It was too late.

We've got to put our phones in a locked cupboard. See you on the other side!!!

She'd even sent a picture of herself posing in front of a set of cubby holes and wearing a comedy worried face. Edee threw the phone to the bed, followed by the glasses. Three days. How could she wait three days to tell her?

16

"I've had the best idea," said Maddie.

It was the next morning and they were heading towards their form room. Edee was a pace behind. She'd put the glasses on a few minutes ago, for the first time since last night, and had been examining the back of Cass's head from her vantage point of half a metre or so away. She couldn't pick out the symbol-line any more than she'd been able to pick out her own previously lettered one. It could have been any one of a thousand, ten thousand, more. In fact, she was beginning to realise that some of the lines were tiny, narrow as pinpricks, and that sometimes several tiny ones near each other glowed at the same time, giving the impression of width. Now, for instance, several groups were glittering down her friend's back.

For the last ten minutes or so, Cass had been going on and on about Ty again. She'd only paused to check her phone for new messages (he'd text twice last night) and that's when Maddie had grabbed the opportunity to speak.

"The best," she said again. "I was thinking about all of us missing Lucie and that there has to be an answer. Then I remembered Mum and Dad are going out on Friday. You can come and stay at mine and we'll call her. She can be there on my laptop. Like an international sleepover."

Cass laughed. "Love it."

"What do you reckon?" said Maddie, turning back. "I've messaged her so she'll get it as soon as they're out. And Mum's already ordered us some food." She slowed and pulled Edee into a hug. "I wanted to cheer you up."

Edee tore her attention from Cass's back. She'd been about to say no, because she wanted to talk to Lucie alone. But she couldn't say no now. She tried to smile like she meant it. "Great, yeah."

Cass turned round, walking backwards. She was beaming. "He text again."

THE HOURS DRAGGED. By the time Friday evening came around, Edee felt like she'd lived through three weeks rather than three days. She'd spent an inordinate amount of time watching in the mirror for new beads to appear around her head. None had, yet she was sure the lines over her seemed thicker. She'd also examined the ones on her arm with a magnifying glass but had learned nothing more. Later, she'd written down everything she knew about the lines so far but had come to no conclusions.

She'd also headed off loads of questions from Mum about jobs, and had spent hours and hours thinking about the next counselling appointment (for whether something else might happen to the lines during it, rather than for what Maggie might go on about). Several times she had got so close to going back to the cafe, but she always stopped herself. The last thing she wanted was for Kitty to think she was creepy.

Lucie had texted as soon as she'd been reunited with her phone. She'd (predictably) loved everything about the retreat and was even more excited than Maddie about the coming evening. All afternoon she updated them on the journey to the newest campsite and every tactic she was employing to stop Rosa and Greg getting distracted by all manner of villages, monuments, and food places. To Edee, it felt like some weird, final countdown to a thing that was simply getting in the way. A thing that was delaying the one thing she wanted. All in all, by the time she knocked on the door just before seven, she felt exhausted.

"Edes!" said Maddie. She was already dressed in pyjamas. They were accessorised with a woolly hat and chunky slipper socks. "A person with actual ears. Cass is on the phone again. Can you believe she wanted to invite him? My mum said no." She lowered her voice. "I asked her to."

Edee smiled, fighting a yawn, and handed over the bags of crisps and popcorn that Mum had bought.

"Thanks." Maddie ripped open the popcorn bag and moved towards the lounge. "We're in here. The kids are at my nan's and Mum and Dad have just left. They won't be back for ages."

The sofa and the floor were both covered with duvets, blankets, and cushions. A few battery-operated candles were scattered in the gaps. Maddie's laptop was set up on a coffee table that was artfully covered in pictures (lined) of the four of them. Cass, also pyjamaed, was curled up in a chair. She raised a hand in greeting before turning away again.

Maddie glanced at the clock. "Five minutes. Do you want to get changed?"

"Sure," said Edee.

"If she's not off the phone when you're done, I'll hold her legs and you can grab it," said Maddie. She headed towards the kitchen with the bag of popcorn still in hand.

Edee returned to the hallway and went into the toilet opposite the lounge, squeezing past the wet weather gear and the plastic box filled with all manner of sports shoes and equipment. A few minutes later, with a cosy jumper pulled on over her pyjamas, she crossed the hall again. Cass's laugh floated through the doorway. Crockery clunked in the kitchen. Edee halted as if some obstacle had emerged from the carpet. The stairway's gallery wall was reflected in the mirror before her and so, therefore, was line after shiny line. She changed direction.

The display wasn't the sort of thing that featured in Mum's magazines. None of the frames matched and neither were they well spaced. Edee, however, cared nothing for that as she climbed step after step. The pictures were a potted history of Maddie's family, showing it expanding from a long-term three to four, five, and six in quick succession. It was also, it turned out, a history of their lines. If only she'd come here last week, she would've seen the baby thing as clear as anything. The pictures were randomly arranged, but it would have been so simple to reorder them chronologically from the way one or other of the children became more lined. Yet, at the same time, it wasn't constant. In fact, seeing them next to each other like this also made the differences in the lines just as obvious. Here and there some of them even looked similar to Kitty's.

Had the lines faded on the paper or had the photos captured them as they'd been? Were they really like Kitty's? Edee leaned forward, her left foot dangling above the lower step. Maddie's family were so normal. They were nothing like Kitty.

"Edes?" said Maddie.

Edee's head snapped to the left and her stomach swooped like she'd missed her footing. "I was . . . just looking."

Something like a frown might have passed across Maddie's face.

"Everything's so, um, clear," said Edee, pointing to the glasses. Her face was getting hot like she'd been caught doing something terrible. That was ridiculous. It was only some pictures. Maddie wouldn't mind. She took one step down and another.

"Lucie said she'll be one minute," said Maddie.

"Okay." Edee reached the hallway. She met Maddie's eyes again. There *was* some kind of odd look on her face except, as she watched, Maddie straightened it out.

"She's ready," called Cass, swinging into the hall around a hand planted on the doorframe. "Edes, I totally owe you for going to the cafe on Tuesday. It's literally changed my life. In three days. It's mad."

Maddie said, "It's girls tonight." She turned and steered Cass back into the lounge. "You can tell us about Ty again tomorrow."

"But I can't think about anything else," said Cass. "I can't believe I've only known him for a few days."

"Think about Lucie," said Maddie. "She's been in a cult for three days."

"It was a retreat," said Cass. She looked over her shoulder and smiled. "Ty's been on a retreat." She held up her hands. "Just saying."

"Can't hear you," said Maddie. "This place is always full of boys. Tonight it's not." She stopped in front of the laptop. Seconds later, Lucie was waving, her shoulders rising and falling at the same time, and her head moving side to side.

Edee's belly twisted with an amplified need to talk to her properly, privately.

"This is the best idea ever." Lucie stopped dancing,

picked up a mug, and raised it to the camera before leaning forward. "Where are yours?"

"We haven't made them yet," said Maddie, kneeling in front of the laptop. "Cass was supposed to be doing it." She prodded Cass's leg. "Can't you pretend you're already working in the cafe or something?" She leaned towards the screen. "Did you manage to get any of the stuff on the list?"

Lucie held up a paper bag.

Cass reached back and grabbed Edee's arm, pulling her towards the kitchen.

NOW AND THEN THE wi-fi signal stuttered. But, punctuated by a few pauses here and there, they ate together, painted their nails, and tried out a few face masks while Lucie narrated what felt like the whole of the retreat. It definitely had not been silent, judging by the amount of information she had picked up about every single person there—Finn, Mal, Flea, the list went on and on.

When she finally slowed down, Cass began talking about Ty, holding a hand out to Maddie. "She said she wants to know *everything* that's going on. I can't leave this out."

Edee's stomach curled over and over. She told herself this was a delay, nothing more, and did her best to look enthusiastic when Cass said how grateful she was to have gone to the cafe and how she owed everything to Edee. From Ty, the conversation wandered back and forth around travelling, the retreat, school, and the various people Lucie had met in the last few weeks. It only stopped because Cass fell asleep.

Maddie yawned. "She was up until two last night. Lightweight."

Lucie grinned.

"We'll call you in the morning for breakfast," said Maddie.

"Can't wait," said Lucie. "Love you." She waved and the picture disappeared.

Maddie rolled onto her side. "I hope it helped a bit, Edes. Cheered you up."

It wasn't as if she could say no, so Edee agreed and then tried to lay as still as possible while Maddie's breathing got softer and softer. One by one the candles dimmed then faltered to nothing. The clock on the mantelpiece ticked on and on, louder and louder. But the exhaustion Edee had felt earlier in the evening refused to give way to a genuine, restful tired. She heard Maddie's parents' car pull up on the gravel, their key in the lock, the lounge door softly opening and closing, and the hushed voices moving upstairs.

She was the last person to fall asleep.

And the first to wake up.

It was still dark, barely seven-thirty, yet she felt wide awake, much too awake to be lying still. Slipping out from the duvet and picking up the glasses, she headed to the toilet and then found herself back at the gallery wall lingering over the lines that looked like Kitty's. She moved up and down the steps searching the pictures and her brain for anything else that might connect them. It was impossible. Maddie's brothers, her parents, and other random relatives were nothing like Kitty. The only thing that linked them was this occasional level of opacity.

And pictures lied. They could lie. Everyone knew that. Any of them might have been manipulated, edited, just like Maddie had done with that one of them. None of this was any help. None at all.

Shivering, Edee crossed her arms around herself and moved back down the steps. It wouldn't be long now before she could go and phone Lucie. Perhaps Lucie would be able to see some connection that she had missed. Perhaps it would be obvious to her. In fact, she might as well get dressed now and then she'd be ready to—

Her body came to an abrupt stop behind the palm that was flat against the half-open lounge door. Her stomach, however, dropped like she had missed some invisible step while her brain flew into overdrive. Neither Maddie nor Cass were covered by their barcodes.

17

Edee glanced down at her body. It was glittering as usual and the pictures had been lined. The glasses must still be working. Even so, she took them off and put them back on again. It didn't make any difference. The two of them were still unlined.

None of the pictures on the wall had shown a grown person without lines.

Crouching beside Maddie, her heartbeat pulsing uncomfortably, she leaned down and peered at her face. It was Maddie's face exactly as she'd known it until a week ago: unlined and un-glittering. She glanced to the side. The duvet was rising and falling. She was breathing.

Edee sat back on her heels, relief mixing with confusion. The room was dimly lit since the curtains were still pulled, but that hadn't made any difference last night. It had been darker then and she'd had no trouble seeing them. It would've been more trouble not to see them. Right now, the lines should be lighting everything up like mini white-light suns. Three of them, not one.

Standing, she carefully stepped across Maddie's body,

avoiding the arm flung out to the side, and picked her way towards Cass who had not moved since she'd fallen asleep mid-call. Kneeling down again, Edee brought her face level with her friend's before turning her head to the side. There was nothing. Not even a hint that anything had ever been there at all.

Cass was curled up so tightly it was impossible to see if she was breathing too. Edee raised the back of her hand and inched it towards Cass's nose. The lightest touch of air brushed across it. A second wave of relief passed through her.

It was short lived.

Cass's eyes opened. She lifted her head and gasped, "Jesus."

Edee reared backwards, tripping over her own feet, and knocking Maddie's outstretched arm.

And the lines covering Cass were back. Instantly back. One moment they hadn't been and then they were. *Now* they were, glittering and shining and creating a light show as if they'd never left.

"Sorry," said Edee, her heart thudding and her head swivelling towards Maddie whose eyes were beginning to open.

"Huh?" said Maddie. "What's going on?"

And her lines crackled into being too. She raised herself up on a folded arm and blearily peered in their direction.

"Edee, giving me a heart attack," said Cass, flopping back down but fixing her with a look of confusion. She brought her hands to her face. "My head. It's totally spinning. God, Edee. What were you doing?"

"Is something wrong?" said Maddie.

"No," said Edee. She could barely concentrate on anything other than the way the lines had come into being. "No, I . . ."

"What?" said Maddie.

"I . . . you made a weird noise," said Edee. Her insides writhed at the new lie. "Like you couldn't breathe. I was seeing if you were okay."

"And you thought you'd stop my heart and make me pee myself instead?" said Cass. She raised her head a touch towards Maddie. "I didn't."

Maddie was looking a little like she had last night by the stairs, but Edee couldn't think about that right now because she was too busy with the connections that were popping inside her head. The lines had appeared the instant they'd both woken up. Those beads of light had been so, so close to the top of her head and to Cass's head. The things were connected to them, part of them. They had to be.

Edee lifted up the glasses.

The lines did not budge.

Her intake of breath was audible. She lowered and raised the glasses over and over as if she'd made some mistake, but nothing changed.

"Edes," said Maddie, rolling sideways then kneeling. "Are you okay? Are you having a panic attack?"

Edee shook her head and somehow managed to talk. "No, I'm fine. I'm—" Both of them were looking at her like there was something wrong, like she was an alien. "I'm, I mean, I'm sorry. I didn't mean to scare you. I . . ."

Cass rubbed her face again then patted the sofa, before pulling her phone from beneath a cushion.

Edee let the glasses drop to her nose one more time before taking them off. It did not make the slightest difference.

"It's not even eight o'clock." Cass flopped down again and curled back up. "It's Saturday."

"You had more sleep than we did," said Maddie. "We were talking and you were gone. Right, Edes?" She was caught somewhere between a frown and an encouraging smile.

"Um," managed Edee. This was huge. Huge.

Maddie shifted a little. "What do you want for breakfast? Pancakes?"

"Mmm," said Cass, closing her eyes. "In a bit."

Edee picked her way to the other side of the room and grabbed her bag. "It's cold. I'm going to get dressed." She was out the door before either of them had a chance to reply. In the toilet, she pulled on her jeans and hoody while trying not to look at the lines over her body. It was impossible, of course, because there was no respite from the shining now.

She rubbed the sides of her head as if that might help her wrap her mind around the sheer absurdity of it all. A few days ago, she'd thought she'd had a handle on this whole thing, and now this had happened. Which meant what? That it wasn't the glasses after all. Or, rather, that it had started as the glasses and now, somehow, it wasn't.

She paused, still as a statue again, as if she was a little kid and someone had turned off the music. It didn't feel wrong. No, it did, but it didn't. It was weird, of course it was, but it didn't feel bad. She wasn't scared. In fact, underneath the surprise, she felt like she had at the cafe with Kitty, that somehow this made sense. Could she . . . was she able to see the lines now because she'd been right? Right about the lines coming from people's own heads and this was some kind of confirmation. A bizarre prize. It seemed peculiar enough to be plausible.

This really was huge. It was way, way too big to keep to herself and she didn't want to. Not at all. In fact, if she'd thought she wanted to talk to Lucie before, well, now it was like the blood running through her body was full of a singular desire. Pulling her phone from the pocket in her bag, she sent a text: *Are you up? Have to speak to you xxx*

Then: *Alone.*

She stared at the thing, hoping some kind of cosmic coincidence had woken Lucie at the same time. Or that the phone's tone had. She'd take either.

A few seconds later Lucie was typing. There was the tiniest delay, before: *Course. Mum and Dad are here. Fifteen mins? xxx*

Edee caught her top lip between her teeth. There she was. Real-Lucie. Dependable, interested, always-there Lucie. She read the text a few more times before slipping back the bolt and heading across the hallway.

The lounge door was not quite closed, and Maddie and Cass were talking in hushed voices. The words were indistinguishable but the subject matter was obvious. Pausing for a second or two, she crept back a few steps, then walked forward and pushed the door open like the last ten minutes had not happened. The hushed voices stopped.

"We decided on pancakes," said Maddie. "With banana and honey. Or there's yogurt and berries, or chocolate spread, whatever you want." This time she spoke with the same over-keen, cajoling tone she sometimes used for her brothers.

"Great," said Edee, making herself meet one set of eyes then the other. "I'd love to, but I've got to go."

"Go?" said Cass. "Go where? It's not even eight."

"I know." Edee clutched her phone. "Mum's just texted and we've got to go and pick up some stuff for her work." It was semi-feasible. They did sometimes do that at the weekend. Both Cass and Maddie, however, were looking unconvinced. Cass had drawn her legs up to sitting. She crossed her arms.

"Is she picking you up?" said Maddie.

109

"Yeah," improvised Edee. "But I'm going to start walking because . . ." She fidgeted with the ball of pyjamas. "Because I want to call Lucie first. There's some stuff I didn't get chance to tell her last night."

"Call her back here." Maddie pointed to the laptop. "Speak to her while we make breakfast."

Edee shook her head. She didn't want them overhearing. Not yet. "I've got to go. There isn't much time. The place is miles away."

There was silence. Maddie broke it with, "Is everything okay?"

Edee nodded, shoving the crumpled pyjamas into her bag at the same time, before pulling the zip across. "Sorry I woke you up and everything. I'll, um, message later." She was back in the hallway, had pulled her shoes on, and was flicking the latch before Maddie made it out of the lounge.

"Edes, are you sure—"

"Yeah. Everything's great," said Edee. "Thanks for last night and everything." She stepped out onto the driveway and checked the time. She had five minutes to get somewhere private.

18

S omewhere private that had wi-fi because she needed to see Lucie too. There wasn't enough time to get home. It was going to have to be a cafe. The one on the crossroads should be open. She scrabbled in the bottom of her bag to see if she had enough change for anything in there. She did. Just.

She ran, only slowing when she could see the cafe's door. Her breath was coming fast. Her back was damp.

Please don't be empty, she thought, pushing the door open. It wasn't, but it wasn't exactly busy either. Checking the time—two minutes to go—she rushed to the counter and scanned the drinks menu on the board.

"Hello there," said the waiter.

Edee held out the pile of change. "Tea, please."

"To have in?" he said.

She nodded.

"Breakfast okay for you?"

She was already starting to move away, scanning the room. "Yeah."

He leaned across, holding out a wooden spoon with

'fourteen' burned into the bowl. "Take a seat. Won't be a moment."

She reached back to take it, then carried on moving towards the booth that was nearest to the front door. It wasn't ideal; there was a table to the side, too close, but it would have to do. Shuffling across the padded seat, she scrabbled in her bag for her headphones. The wi-fi password hadn't changed since she'd been here with Maddie.

Seconds later, Lucie was calling. Edee swiped the screen.

"Hey," said Lucie. "What's up?"

Edee twisted, wedging herself into the corner. The tall, squashy back of the booth was to her left side and the wall was to her right. She'd be able to see anyone approaching the table.

"Edes?" said Lucie. "Can you hear me?"

"Hi," said Edee. She spoke in little more than a whisper. "Are you on your own?"

Lucie nodded. "They've gone off for a walk. I told them you were upset."

Edee chewed her lip. Lucie's lines were glittering. She lifted the glasses a couple of centimetres. They still glittered.

"I had to tell them something," said Lucie. "It was all I could think of. Sorry."

"It's okay." Edee didn't care what Rosa and Greg thought. They were out of the way. That was the important thing.

"What is it?" Lucie looked intrigued. "What's happened? Why aren't you at Maddie's?"

Now that the moment was here, Edee wasn't exactly sure where to start. She glanced up one more time—no one was near—then focused on Lucie's glittering face again. There was nothing for it but to start talking. It was Lucie, after all. Even so, her toes inexplicably curled in her shoes before she began. "This weird stuff's been happening."

"Weird?" said Lucie, leaning in. "Did you say weird?"

"Yeah."

"Oooh," said Lucie. "What kind of weird?"

"Weird, weird," said Edee. "Wait, no, that's not right. It started off weird, but it isn't anymore. It's . . . got better. It's better than weird."

Lucie grinned. "Brilliant."

Edee glanced up. No one was near. "It started when I got my glasses."

"I knew there was something." Lucie's eyebrows moved to peaks above the grin. "But you wouldn't say."

"Yeah, well I didn't get it then," said Edee. "I still don't, not completely."

"What? You've got, like, x-ray vision now?" said Lucie, the grin becoming toothy.

Edee looked up and around again. The coast was still clear. "This is private, right?"

"Yeah." The intrigue was back on Lucie's face, more intense. "There's only me here and the door's shut. I can shut the window it you like, although I might boil."

"No, it's alright," said Edee. She paused. "But you can't tell anyone, okay. Promise."

"Edes, it's me," said Lucie. "Go on."

There was a noise. A couple of grey-haired people were hovering on the other side of the door, reading the menu. Even though they were outside, Edee lowered her whisper a fraction more. "It's, well, ever since I got them, I've been able to see something. Something I couldn't see before."

"It is x-ray vision?" said Lucie. She laughed. "No way."

Edee shook her head, willing her to take this seriously.

Lucie's face straightened. "Okay, not that. You mean it's more than stuff being clearer?"

Edee nodded.

"What?" said Lucie. "What are you seeing?"

113

"Lines."

"Lines?" Lucie said the word like she'd never heard it before.

The waiter appeared by the table. He smiled, putting down the mug and the milk jug. Edee passed him the wooden spoon. Why was he lingering? Couldn't he see she was busy? She looked away. A bell on the front door tinkled. The grey-haired couple were coming in. He turned to greet them.

"What sort of lines?" said Lucie. "Fuzzy? Do you mean they're making you see worse?"

Edee shook her head and waited until the three people moved past before whispering again. "I can see fine. They're only over people."

"People?" said Lucie. "Over people?"

"Yeah."

"What people? Who?"

"Everyone, pretty much."

"Everyone?" Lucie looked up and down. "Me?"

"Yeah."

"What kind of lines?"

"Ones that glitter. They go all the way around. It's like you—*people*—are wrapped up inside them. They're sort of like see-through wrapping paper. You know the stuff that's around bunches of flowers? But stripy and kind of animated. It's not one piece though, it's made up of the lines."

"Cellophane that moves?" said Lucie. She wrinkled her nose. "Eeugh. What did the optician say?"

Edee shook her head. "Nothing. I didn't say anything when I got them. I was, I don't know, too surprised and everything else had been so weird as well that I just didn't. Then it was too late, and afterwards I thought that if I went back they might take them off me and I didn't want them to. I wanted to know what they are."

"How do you know they're anything?" said Lucie. "We aren't covered in lines. They must be faulty."

"I thought that too." Edee shuffled even further into the corner, wishing Lucie would hurry up and get it so she could tell her about today's developments. "But people's lines look different. If it was the glasses then everyone would look the same, wouldn't they."

Lucie tilted her head to the side. "Are they scratched? Is it double vision?"

"No." Edee shook her head at the same time as if to answer both questions at once. "They're only around people. If it was double vision or scratches they'd be over everything."

There was a pause, then Lucie said, "Are you saying you can see lines on me now?"

"Yeah," said Edee.

Lucie patted her face, like she was trying to feel something. "There's nothing."

"There is," said Edee. Her friend looked confused but she pressed on anyway. "And the thing is, after a few days, I realised that little kids, babies, don't have them. You know when we were talking the other day and that family went by . . ."

Recognition flashed across Lucie's face. "I knew it. I knew there was something weird about that. When you said the baby was cute—"

"That's when I realised," said Edee. "And also that it's not only here, like geographically. It's everywhere. You have them in France, and my dad does too. Then, the other day, I saw a line appear. It sort of grew from someone's head."

Lucie's face crumpled. "Grew?"

"Yeah. I saw it. Twice. And the thing is, today I realised . . . I think we make them."

"Make them?" said Lucie. "Hang on. Are you saying it actually, sort of, came out of someone's head like a . . . like a flower? A weed? No, wait, like hair?"

"Yeah. Well, kind of. I saw it above their head. One moment it wasn't there and then it was, this bead of light. It circled their whole body, leaving a sort of trail, and joined up with itself at the top to make a new line."

"Then what happened?" said Lucie.

"It glowed for a bit and looked like all the others. Shiny —the lines shine—and I couldn't see which it was after it joined up. So the others must've got there in the same way. They're really close together. That's what makes it look like a sheet."

"You're making it sound like some kind of alien thing," said Lucie. "You don't mean that . . . do you?"

"No," said Edee. "I mean, I did think that for a bit, but it isn't." Her heartbeat was speeding up again because here it was at last. She could almost taste the relief of the words she was about to say. "Because something else happened this morning. That's what I wanted to tell you, why I messaged. When Cass and Maddie were asleep, they had nothing and as soon as they woke up, they did. I think people make them, but they don't know. When they're asleep they forget or something."

"Make them?" said Lucie. "Why? Why would anyone do that?"

"They don't know they are," said Edee. "I didn't." It was easy to talk about this after all. So easy, as if everything about the lines had been queued up in her brain waiting to pour out. "There's more. When I realised about making them, I was able to see the lines without the glasses at all."

She lifted them up. "When I look at you now, you're still covered."

In the screen, the lines weren't quite as clear—defined—as they would be in real face-to-face life, but they were clear enough. If only she could draw them or something. That would make it easier for Lucie to get it. Maybe she could get a photo and put lines over that with some silver pen or some glitter. More than anything she wanted Lucie to understand what it looked like and how fascinating it all was.

Lucie, however, was not looking fascinated. Not at all. Several more lines around her were shining. "Edes, you're saying you're seeing things?"

"Yes," said Edee. "No. I mean yes, but not in a bad way. I thought it might be to begin with because I didn't know what it was. Now I think it's telling me something. I think it's important. Big. Something I'm supposed to know."

Lucie sat back. Her face was a little less scrunched, but her eyebrows were still pointing like arrows towards her hairline.

"I'm not making it up," said Edee.

"I don't think you could." Lucie's phone dropped a bit and the picture went wonky for a few seconds. "Has anyone else tried them on? What have they said?"

Edee shook her head. "Mum tried them and so did Cass. They said they couldn't see anything at all; it was too blurry. They don't have the same prescription as me."

Lucie was looking directly at the camera now. "Edes, this is . . ."

"I know." Even with Lucie being slow to catch on, it was so much better to have told someone. No, not someone, *her*. "I'm sorry I didn't say anything before. It was so weird that I was trying to figure it out a bit first. And you had so much on. Every time we spoke, your parents were around or someone else was."

"I'm glad you've told me now," said Lucie slowly. "What are you going to do? Are you going to tell your mum?"

"No." This could have been the moment to tell Lucie about the counselling. Except it wasn't because . . . it wasn't. Because she didn't have anything to say about that. The glasses were way, way more interesting. Besides, Lucie knew Mum. In fact, saying she should tell her was a stupid thing to say. She'd realise that in a minute. "Mum'd only worry, and I want to find out more. I only realised the part about sleeping this morning. And it hasn't even been an hour since I could see them without the glasses. I'm going to notice so much more now. I won't be able to help but notice stuff. I'll probably have it figured out in a few days."

"Yeah," said Lucie. "I guess. Edes, it's . . ."

Even with the look on Lucie's face, Edee couldn't help but smile. Her best friend was lost for words. That hardly ever happened. In fact, she looked a bit lost. It could have been disorientating. Except, of course . . . *of course.*

It was always Lucie's family who were doing new stuff. They'd done nothing but new stuff for two weeks and here she was surrounded by fascinating, off the chart, new and different, having not asked for it at all. It was upside down and that was there, plain as could be, on Lucie's face. She was wishing this had happened to her. She was jealous. Jealous of her. Edee softened. "I'll tell you everything I find out about it. I promise. There's going to be loads."

Lucie nodded slowly. "You have to. Every single thing."

Edee laughed. It came from deep within. "Of course I will. Anyway, what are you doing today?"

"Good," said Lucie. She looked away from the camera for a few seconds, like something else was trying to catch her attention. "We're driving into Italy."

"Italy?" said Edee. "Pizzas. Ice cream. Old stuff."

"Yeah," said Lucie, looking back. "Listen, I think you should tell your mum about the lines."

"No," said Edee, shaking her head. Mum would freak out. It was beyond obvious. Why was Lucie being slower than slow?

"You're seeing things," said Lucie. "That's—"

"I'm not," said Edee.

"But you said—"

"Not like that. Not *seeing* stuff, bad. I think it's something that's there but that people normally can't see. Like you can't see it now. It's good that I can. It's—"

"But that's . . ."

Wait. Had she got this wrong? Had Lucie actually misunderstood? The whole point of telling her was to have someone to talk to about this, to share the enormity of it all, not . . . this.

"Then I think you should go back to the optician's," said Lucie. "You just said that it isn't the glasses after all. What if there's something wrong with your eyes now? What if the glasses have broken them?" She was leaning so far forward, the whole screen was taken up with her face. Her shining, glittering, frowning face.

"No, there is a reason," said Edee. "That's what I'm saying. I just don't know what it is yet. Not my eyes. Something else. Bigger. I am seeing things, yeah, but it's good. I want to be."

The moment the end of the sentence left her mouth, she had the same feeling she'd had in Mr Millard's classroom. The cafe had been quiet before, now it was silent. The grey-haired couple had taken seats by the window and they were both staring at her. The woman looked away, awkward. Edee had the awful feeling she'd said those words too loud and they, of course, would not understand. Not at all. They'd probably try and . . . grabbing her bag, she wriggled from the seat. Her knee hit the table leg and the cooling tea sloshed from the mug. Now the waiter was heading towards her. She fled to the door, opening it with one finger, dashed through, and ran from the place.

She was several shops away when she realised her phone was still in her hand. The picture of Lucie was blurred behind a poor connection message and now she was voice calling. Edee left the thing buzzing in her hand as she glanced behind, then turned down a side street.

19

Old-Lucie wouldn't have said that. She just wouldn't. Had she said it because she was jealous or because she'd really changed? Edee's feet pounded the tarmac to the beat of everything that was running through her mind.

Her phone buzzed again, interrupting. A text this time. *What happened? Were you running? Call me xxx*

She carried on moving, her mind now whirring faster than her feet. Lucie had seemed interested and then . . . that. Of course she wasn't going to tell Mum. Not with the counselling and the friend thing. The lines were different, she got that. And perhaps she had thrown the whole thing at her, but she was Lucie. She was supposed to be, well, *Lucie*.

The phone rang again. She did not answer. There was another flurry of messages.

Are you okay?
What's happening?
Why aren't you answering? xxx

This time, Edee stopped and began typing. *Everything's*

fine. Had to leave the café. Will call later. Don't worry about the other stuff. Forget I told you. It's fine. Maybe I got it wrong xx

She hit send, then began moving again. The bag on her shoulder suddenly felt a lot heavier and spots of rain began spattering the ground. She pulled the hood up on her jumper. She had not got it wrong.

Her phone buzzed once more. *I can't forget. I want to help. Call me xxx*

Wiping the screen on her jeans, she shoved it into her bag. One, two, three streets went by in a haze of watery grey tarmac before she looked up again—up towards another barcode in front of her . . . that had just disappeared, like the girl's in the park. She stared. It came back. The man inside was way, way older than the girl had been. And that person over there, on the opposite side of the road, was covered more thickly than Craig had been. She slowed, barely registering the rain that continued to soak her jumper and her hood. Those people moved off and new ones came into view. Their lines were different again.

A GOOD HALF AN HOUR LATER, Edee put her key in the lock and eased open the front door to the apartment. She paused, listening. Her whole being felt like it was overflowing with everything the morning had thrown her way, including the sheer variety of lines she had seen in the last thirty minutes. The very last thing she needed was an interrogation from Mum about why she'd returned before breakfast. Had it not turned torrential out there she would've happily stayed out for ages yet, but the water had started to run down her neck. If only she'd taken an umbrella. If only she could grab that one on the coat stand and head back out. She took a step towards it and stopped.

The office chair was rattling over the floorboards. Mum poked her head into the hallway. "You're back early." She rotated a little. "You're soaking."

Edee nodded, retreating onto the doormat.

"Is everything alright?" The lines over Mum's head and shoulders were glittering.

"Yep," said Edee, torn between wanting and not wanting to watch them.

"Are you sure?" said Mum. "Why didn't you call for a lift? Where were Maddie's parents? Why didn't they drop you back?"

"I walked," said Edee, slipping off her sodden shoes. "I wanted to speak to Lucie. It wasn't raining when I left."

"I thought speaking to Lucie was the whole reason you stayed over," said Mum.

"Yes." Edee tried to look normal. Her face felt anything but. "Cass and Maddie were there. Someone else is always around now. If it's not someone here, it's Rosa and Greg."

Mum opened her mouth to say something then shut it again. She pressed her lips together for a couple of seconds then said, "Have a hot drink or a hot shower or something to warm up."

Edee turned on the spot and headed to her room. That was it? She would take that. She would take it with bells on.

"By the way," said Mum. "Craig, Scotty, and Amber are coming for dinner tonight. That's alright by you, isn't it?"

Edee paused, one hand on the doorframe. Half of her was thinking no, not tonight, while the other half could not help but think it would be more time to study their lines and actually that was . . . good. She glanced back and tried to sound casual. "Okay."

AN HOUR OR SO LATER, the two of them were outside the supermarket. It was the same one they'd come to after the optician's appointment. A lifetime ago.

"We'll run in and out," said Mum. "Shopping at the weekend is madness but it can't be helped. They deserve to have a good evening."

Edee clutched the basket. She'd agreed to come here without realising. Freshly showered, she'd been too busy looking out the window at all the lines down on the street below and had muttered an "mmm" to Mum's invitation. Now they were weaving their way through the people in fruit and veg and the whole experience—the supermarket— was feeling otherworldly. On any other day, this would've been the most boring place ever of course, yet today it was anything but.

She'd thought, for instance, that this morning's feast of lines had been interesting—they had been—but the sheer number of them here was something else. They even seemed *more*, somehow, than they had that day in the park when she'd had the first inkling into the scale of the thing. Maybe it was because there was no frame limiting the vision in front of her now, or maybe it was something to do with the shining underneath the artificial lights in the shop's expanse. Whatever the reason, it was like she was swimming through lines and her attention was darting from one to the next, watching that one glitter ahead and then that one shining to the side. At the same time, however, a bigger realisation was beginning to unfold. Disappearing lines, it was turning out, were not unusual at all. She'd thought there had been something special about that girl in the park, but so far she'd seen three or four people's lines completely disappear. Always fleeting, yes, but it happened. It was happening. Which meant what? Were people falling asleep while they were going about their day? Surely not. Their eyes were open. They were moving. And yet—

"Edee?"

Her eyes took a second to catch up as she turned, and then another second to focus. Her stomach, the one that had been surprisingly calm for a while, plummeted. It was Maddie—a confused-looking Maddie—standing between her and Mum, who was reading the back of some bottle of oil a few paces away.

"Hi," murmured Edee.

Two of Maddie's brothers were with her. One was twisting this way and that like a small coil of energy. The other was standing still. Quiet. His eyes were big, as if he too might have been in the middle of some kind of expansive, unpredictable experience.

"What happened to your trip?" said Maddie. There was surprise in her voice and something else that Edee did not want to dwell on.

"It, um, changed," said Edee. Her plummeting stomach writhed at the newest lie. "Sorry. It was too late to come back and I was . . ."

Maddie gave an unconvincing nod.

"Soaked," said Edee. At least that part was true. "I got soaked walking so I went home and then we ended up here." It sounded flimsy. It sounded nothing. "Sorry," she added again.

Maddie's expression had not changed. The big-eyed brother (Micky? Mac? It was hard to tell them apart) was gripping her hand.

"Hello there," said Mum, putting the bottle into the basket. "I hear the sleepover was a success."

"Yeah" said Maddie. "It was . . ."

There was a silence. Edee's brain was filling it with all the questions that would be brewing in Mum's head right now. She shifted the basket, grasping for something to say. "It was really good. Lucie loved it. She, um, told me this morning."

"Good," said Maddie. Her eyes finally softened. "I knew you were missing her and—"

"Yeah," said Edee. No, not that. Not right now. "It was great. Thanks again. You should come and stay at ours sometime."

Maddie nodded. The softened look had changed into something else, something injured. "Sure." She glanced at her brothers. "I'd better go. Dad's here somewhere. He'll be wondering where we are."

"Bye," said Edee.

Mum was lingering, watching Maddie and the two boys walk away.

"Oil, done," said Edee, loudly. Too loudly. "What's next?"

"Mmm?" said Mum. "Oh, rice. Arborio."

Half-way to the next aisle Edee's phone buzzed in her pocket. It was Cass. *What's going on?*

There was also another from Lucie and a couple more missed calls. *Where are you? Phone me xxx*

She shoved the thing back in her pocket. It was starting to feel like she'd somehow fallen into an invisible river and the current was whipping her along, while all around her intense, stronger-than-mid-summer sunlight glinted and gleamed on the surface of the water.

20

When they got back, Edee shoved her phone into her bag and left the bag in her room. It wasn't the answer, she knew that, but it was an answer for now. Mum asked her to help with food preparation and Edee did not complain. In fact, she threw herself into the whole thing, even suggesting they had a go at the smoothies as well. It was a genuine (if a little tightrope) busy and she asked a ton of questions about the recipes so that Mum didn't ask any questions about Maddie or, for that matter, questions about anything else. Despite the busyness, the texts from Lucie and Cass, and the look on Maddie's face, lurked at the edges of her mind. By the time the doorbell went at half six, it seemed like the afternoon had sped by while also, nonsensically, having gone on for days.

"Could you get it?" said Mum, lifting the lid on the saucepan and giving the risotto another stir. She glanced at the recipe once more. "Lemon and Parmesan next. We're almost there."

Edee headed along the hallway, allowing herself to watch the lines of light glittering and glowing over her body.

She opened the door and did a double-take. Scotty was standing there holding the baby who was clutching the cord of his hoody and beaming.

"Dad hasn't done a runner," said Scotty. "Although, let's be honest, who knows? He said he was going to get the other bags. He might be scarpering to the airport." He hoisted Amber up a little. With her so close, his barcode's existence only seemed all the more there.

"Come in," said Edee, standing back.

Amber giggled, then began chewing the cord.

"No," said Scotty, pulling it from her mouth. "There'll be something she can gnaw in there." He pointed a foot at the bag on the mat. "Or you can take her and I'll get it." He held the baby out and Edee, for the first time in her life, took hold of a tiny, squidgy human being. She was heavier than she looked and it occurred to Edee that, even this near, and aside from the size, there was no way she could ever have known the baby was different to any other person. Peering down, she double checked. There was no hint of a line covering her.

Scotty had picked up the bag and was pulling the squeaky giraffe from it. "Here, chew that."

"Hello Scotty," said Mum, at the other end of the hall. "And Amber, cutie. Where's your dad?"

"Gone back down to the car," said Scotty. He raised his eyebrows a little. Edee—impossibly for today, except *not impossibly*—found a smile beginning to form. She bit the inside of her cheek. "To get more stuff," he added. "She doesn't travel light."

"Of course," said Mum. "You'll be ready for sleep soon, Amber, won't you?"

The baby chewed the giraffe.

"He brought the travel cot," said Scotty.

"Lovely," said Mum. "Come through and get a drink." She disappeared back into the kitchen.

Scotty glanced at Edee and Amber, then he shrugged, grinned, and followed her.

Edee pushed the door with an elbow and hesitated for a moment before heading into the lounge. She put the baby on the floor, where she'd been last time they were here. Amber looked up with big, open eyes. She did not seem at all bothered by the fact she was with someone she barely knew or, for that matter, in a place she knew just as little. But she must know that her mum wasn't about.

Scotty reappeared with a glass of the lemonade Mum had decanted into a jug earlier. "That was for leaving me hanging. Virtually."

"Huh?"

"The text. Double conspiracy. Unless it wasn't you after all."

In the restaurant. Oh. She focused on the baby again. "Yeah. It was. I meant to reply. It's been crazy. More crazy. I sort of . . ."

"Forgot?" said Scotty.

"Yes," said Edee. "Sorry."

"It's okay," said Scotty. "I had phone-fighting parents as a distraction."

"Sorry," said Edee again.

"I'm kidding," he said. "Although they were. I'm disappointed they weren't more inventive if I'm honest. They say the same thing over and over."

"Right," said Edee. It wasn't as if she had much experience of fighting parents. Hers had always fought over email.

"Hello," said Craig, appearing in the doorway then taking a couple of steps into the lounge. He was out of breath and wiped his forehead on the palm of his hand.

The lines around him were not far off the intensity they'd been the other day.

Edee found herself staring. He'd *made* them.

"Good to see you again," Craig added. His face was pointed in her direction, but his eyes were glazed. "Kind of your mum to invite us. I'll just set up the cot." He turned around and headed back out with a set of small, busy steps.

"That," said Scotty, "has been happening a lot. Luckily, I've had awesome text communication to keep me going."

Edee opened her mouth, another sorry already beginning to form.

"Kidding," said Scotty.

She shut it.

Amber gave a burbling giggle. She'd started crawling again and the giraffe was poking from her fist.

"Stupid question," said Edee. "But she's missing your mum? I mean, she knows she's not around?"

"Yeah," said Scotty. "Despite appearances and her pathetic vocabulary she's actually pretty switched on. Sometimes it bothers her and she cries. Then again, she cries when her teeth hurt or when her nappy stinks so you could take your pick. You might get a demo soon. She sounds like a siren when she gets started."

Edee nodded.

"Dad's decided it's some kind of post-natal depression," said Scotty. "Mum going, not the siren."

Several lines were glittering over his body. Edee couldn't have sworn to it, but she was fairly sure at least a few of them were new. She tried to concentrate on the conversation. "It might be?"

"I guess," said Scotty. "But I think he's delusional. She can't get enough of Reg. Which is not something I need to know about my mother." He screwed up his face.

AN HOUR OR SO LATER, the four of them were around the table in the kitchen finishing off the fancy ice cream Mum had picked out that morning. Amber was asleep in the travel cot in the lounge. Craig had been jumping up to check on her every fifteen minutes or so.

"Coffee?" said Mum, as he stood up again. "Why don't you go and sit with Amber and I'll bring it through. You two can stay here if you like. You can be noisier in here, obviously."

"Sure," said Scotty. His eyes lit up and the flicker of a smile flashed over his face.

Craig disappeared and Mum busied herself with the coffee machine and the ice cream bowls.

"Subtle," Scotty mouthed to Edee.

Yep. About as subtle as the lines that were covering Craig.

The two of them didn't say much while the coffee machine whirred. Then Mum picked up the two cups and headed towards the doorway. At the last moment she indicated the leftovers with a nod of her head. "Help yourself to any more food."

They heard her elbowing the lounge door closed.

"I think you're now supposed to offer me moral support over the warring state of my parents," said Scotty. "Loudly."

Edee chewed her lip.

"Or not," he added. "I'm fairly sure there are other things going on in the world." He pulled his phone from his pocket.

She wasn't sure if he was bored or trying to tell her they didn't have to say a word to each other. The thing was, all of a sudden, she wanted to. More than that, a question had arrived fully formed and now she was saying it, as if the words had an energy of their own; as if, finally, she was ready—*able*—to pay some attention to everything that had gone on today. "Do you ever feel like there's stuff going on that you don't know about?"

"Like my mum getting it on with some bloke from my dad's work while we were playing happy families?" said Scotty. "I would say so, yeah."

Edee tried to hold back the blood that was rushing to her cheeks. "No, I didn't mean that. I meant bigger stuff." Wait, no, his mum leaving was big. "Not bigger, sort of epic stuff that goes on and we have no idea about because we can't see it." Usually, she added in her head.

The change in his face was quite something. His eyes sparkled so much they showed up clear against all the other light around him. "Course." It was emphatic, almost as if he'd been waiting to be asked or something. Which he hadn't been, obviously. No one would be waiting for that. "Otherwise how do birds fly?"

Oh. Her stomach plummeted and a single word came to her mind. It was one you had in your brain if you had a dad like hers and it was not relevant to the other stuff. "Thermals."

"Yeah," said Scotty. "For the actual flying. But thermals don't explain how birds migrate, do they? Like swallows and nightingales and stuff. They have their own sat-nav inside their wings or their heads or something."

Wait, he was winding her up? He was some kind of birdwatcher? Scotty? No. But the sparking in his eyes, the emphatic way he'd spoken, he was serious. He did get it. He got something. The shine, however, was fading fast.

He glanced at the phone in his hand again. "You didn't mean that."

"No," said Edee. "No, I did. I didn't think you'd . . ." What? Be interested? Care? Yet the question had come out of her mouth. "I . . . what would you do if you could see it? The whatever it is the birds see. What if you could see silver threads trailing behind them, reaching back to all the places they'd been, or . . ." Now she'd gone too far. He was going to think she'd—

"You mean if I genetically mutated and turned part avian?" said Scotty. The flicker of a smile returned. "Maybe impress people with my navigating skills? Although they'd just think it was sat-nav, wouldn't they? Mmm, I'd make an awesome documentary, showing people how they do it."

"You wouldn't freak out?" said Edee. Lucie telling her to go back to the optician's and to tell Mum was freaking out. And it *still* did not make any sense. Lucie loved new stuff, different stuff. Yet she'd freaked.

"No." Scotty put his phone on the table and leaned the side of his head on his palm. "I'd have a superpower. Why would I freak out?"

Edee shrugged. "Some people would."

"Stupid people," said Scotty. "People who shouldn't get a superpower in the first place."

There was a little part of her that wanted to agree with him and, more, to hold on to that. Lucie had made a mistake. And yet, Lucie wasn't stupid. Not at all. Scotty's lines were glowing and glittering.

"What would you do?" he said.

Edee chewed her lip again. "I don't know."

"You asked the question," said Scotty. "You must have an answer."

Yeah. A non-hypothetical one. "I'd be confused."

He laughed. "Sure. But then what?"

"Then," said Edee, "I'd hope someone would believe me." My best friend, she thought. Her eyes tingled.

"Why would you want someone to believe you?" said Scotty.

"What?" The moisture that had been threatening to cloud Edee's vision disappeared back into her body.

"Why would you care?" Scotty lifted his head from his palm and opened his fingers towards the ceiling. "You'd have a superpower. Why would you bother caring what anyone else thought?"

"Because," said Edee. "Because . . . they should." The morning loomed in her head. The way Lucie had reacted, the things she'd said, the expressions she'd made. It might as well have been happening right then, it was so clear.

Scotty was looking at her like that was the most lame thing he'd ever heard. The lines over him were glittering as much as they had been before. In fact, they looked as if they were playing out some kind of tune, one whose notes she could not quite hear.

"You're saying that if you got a superpower, the first thing you'd want to know is whether someone believed you had one?" he said.

She nodded.

"That's mad."

"It's not mad." Edee's body was glittering as much as his was. It struck her again how she could only see it when she looked down, that she wasn't looking *through* lines.

"It is," said Scotty.

Edee shook her head. "If you suddenly started seeing stuff that was bigger than anything you'd seen before, you'd want someone to believe you." Not someone, specific people. A specific person.

"No you wouldn't," said Scotty, shaking his head a touch. "You'd want to see the bigger stuff. Otherwise you'd spend all your time talking about it and then you might as well not have seen it in the first place."

No, thought Edee.

"Think about it." Scotty shifted, lifting one of his feet to the seat of the chair. "The most interesting thing in your whole life has happened. You'd be so busy living it that you wouldn't care about anything else."

Edee shook her head again. And then said, "Like Amber."

"What?" said Scotty. "What's she got to do with anything?"

"She's . . ." It was like a moth had appeared in Edee's head; a fluttery ghost moth that retreated into the shadows every time she tried to look at it. Amber was relevant. She already knew that. All the babies were. They were unlined. The lines had words when they appeared. They came out of people's heads. The ghost moth fluttered out of sight again, then, of its own accord, settled. "She's free. Freer."

"How do you work that out?" said Scotty. "She can't walk. Or fly. She's not a bird. An avian one."

"No," said Edee, "but she's . . ."

"A baby," said Scotty. "Loud. Chewy. Dribbly. Sometimes cute. Any of them? She's not that interesting."

Edee shook her head. "She's different."

"Sure," said Scotty. "She's small, doesn't speak yet, and moves about on all fours. Are you saying she's got a superpower? If she has, she's keeping it quiet. Unless it's the siren wail. A noise to raise the dead." He reached for his phone again and spun it on the table. "Which would be the worst superpower ever."

Edee bit her lip.

"I like her really," said Scotty. "Most of the time." A different looked flashed across his face. "Are you saying you think she's Reg's not Dad's?"

"No!" Edee was surprised into looking right at him. How had he got there from that? "No, I—"

"I thought the same," said Scotty, slumping a bit. "But sometimes she looks like Dad."

"I didn't mean that." It hadn't even crossed her mind. "I meant . . ." In her head it was making sense, but it was hard to explain. "She's sort of open."

Scotty looked up again. "Open for what?"

For what or to what? "To everything."

"She doesn't have much choice," said Scotty. "She doesn't know much. Her head's kind of empty."

"Mmm," said Edee. It wasn't that.

"Why are you so interested in her?" said Scotty. "Do you want to be a baby when you grow up?" He screwed up his face. "No, that's weird. I didn't say that."

"No," said Edee. She lightly tapped a couple of fingertips on the table. "It's just interesting, that's all. How she's different. How we used to be like her and . . . now we're not."

"She's a baby," said Scotty, getting up and taking the ice cream tub from the side. "Let's get back to the superpowers. They're more interesting."

21

Almost as soon as the three visitors left, Edee found her mind fully occupied again by Lucie and the others. In fact, it wasn't simply back. It was back in microscopic detail and accompanied by a weight that was pressing on her stomach. She could not ignore the three of them forever. They needed some kind of an explanation, or rather Cass and Maddie did and Lucie would need something else. She was going to have to say something. But not yet.

Heading into the lounge, she curled up in the bucket chair. Mum was already on the sofa. The day's news was playing out on the TV. Edee lowered her head as a new, more intense feeling of inescapability circled her like a cloak. That wasn't the news, the real news. She tugged the cushion from behind her and wrapped her arms around it. What if she told Mum about everything right now? What if she spilled it out, line after line? She shook her head. Mum would freak out. Edee had known that from the very instant she'd seen the glittering around the optician's body. Around Mum's body.

But she *could* tell her.

No. Lucie had freaked out and she should've been the interested one. If that was her reaction, Mum's would be unimaginable. The edges of Edee's lips turned a fraction downwards. So yeah, she could tell her if she wanted everything to get even more complicated than it was. It would be easier to rewind her whole life to before that Thursday in the optician's. If only she could go back to when things were simpler, to the time before Rosa had got fixated on travelling. It was like a wall had been built, bisecting life into before and after. Why had she never realised how simple everything was back then, on the before side of the wall?

Mum sighed and Edee hugged the cushion a bit tighter, glancing over. Mum wasn't actually watching the TV. She was staring into space and tracing a finger along the seam on the sofa's arm. The lines around her were glittering and fizzing. It made for an odd picture. Mum, other than her finger, was completely stationary but the lines were like an electrical storm running over her person.

If only Edee could capture this picture, this exact picture, and send it to Lucie and the others, then they'd be interested. For the millionth time, she wondered why she'd got the glasses. Could it have been some kind of chosen one thing?

No. She'd just got a pair of glasses.

Just.

Mum sighed again, then stood up, and turned off the TV before returning the remote to the shelf. "I'm going to have a shower. It's getting late."

Edee didn't reply and Mum disappeared. It was getting late, yet still she did not know what to say to the others. If only she could stay here in the bucket chair and the whole thing would go away. If only someone else could time travel into the past and bulldoze the wall. If only, if only, if only.

She brushed a finger and thumb across her eyelashes. How could something be so fascinating and so difficult at the same time? Along the hallway, the shower began humming.

As soon as Edee entered her room, her attention was drawn to the bag, as if Lucie's prediction of x-ray vision had come true. She turned her back on it, set down the glass of water she'd picked up on the way, and changed into her pyjamas. But turning her back on it was not going to help.

One message, that's all she needed to send. The lines circling her body flickered and glittered some more. She found herself crouching by the bag. For the first time ever, she wished her phone would be broken.

It wasn't. Far from it. There were multiple missed calls from Lucie as well as a collection of texts. The ones from Lucie were variations of, *I'm worried, call me*. The ones from Cass were versions of, *what's going on?* There was nothing from Maddie. Despite everything, nothing was worse. Maddie had been trying to help. She'd looked so injured in the supermarket. A wave of guilt engulfed Edee.

She opened the group message and began typing. *Sorry, hard to explain. Mum's plans changed and we had people for dinner. Everything's fine, really xxx*

Her stomach flipped as she tapped send, but it was done. She stood, wishing she could feel relief instead of this unsettled thing, and made her way into bed, turning off the light as she went and placing her phone face down on the shelf. Even downwards, however, it gave a glow to the room and moments later, when it went to sleep, the darkness seemed deep and thorough. She hadn't cleaned her teeth. She couldn't be bothered to move.

When a reply arrived, Edee sensed the change in light through her eyelids. She tried to pretend she was going to ignore it until the morning. One solitary minute went by before she reached out. She stared. It wasn't Lucie or Cass, it was Scotty. She felt a similar level of surprise as the first time he'd texted her. So much, in fact, that it took her an age before she actually opened the message. When she did, there were two words: *Hey. Awake?*

She found herself typing: *Yeah.*

Good, he said. *You know the superpower thing, they aren't super-powers, just senses. Different ones.*

Okay, she put this time. He'd used that word, not her. But if you could see something that no one else was able to, then didn't that make it a superpower? Or plain weird. Except, weird or not, it was useful. She knew it was. So that did make it a superpower, didn't it?

Senses we don't have, came his next message. *Bird sat-nav is magnetoreception.*

A link to a page all about it popped up below his words. However, before Edee could start reading, he'd messaged again. *Everything would look totally different to us if we were birds but we wouldn't know. Birds must look at us in cars and aeroplanes and think we're mad.* Then, a moment later: *Fish in water. I never got that before.*

Yeah, thought Edee. Impulsively she typed: *Fish in water, birds in air, humans in . . . ?*

Mmm, came Scotty's reply. *Maybe we should ask birds and fish? Better hope for the genetic mutation.*

Edee smiled.

Also, how come humans can't breathe water if it's got oxygen in it? wrote Scotty. *Life's weird.*

Life and parents, replied Edee.

He sent back a laughing face. Then, *And Ambers.*

No. Amber was not weird.

There was a pause before he began typing something else. He stopped and started again.

Another message notification popped up. Lucie this time, direct. Edee's stomach clenched and she read: *It's not fine. You told me you're seeing things and you're not calling me back. Edee, please.*

Now Scotty's message appeared. She flicked back to that one. *The senses thing, the epic stuff we can't see . . . not hypothetical?*

Edee stared, her eyes widening. Her stomach had never felt the things it was feeling now. It was like opposing reactions had run into each other at a million miles an hour. How was it possible to feel this much wrong and this much relief at the same time? It *wasn't* possible, and that's where her stomach was now, stirred up with the impossibility that, for the second time in the past few weeks, she knew exactly what to say to Scotty and not at all what to say to Lucie.

She replied to Scotty first with a simple: *Yes.*

His reply was just as simple: *Awesome. Tell me more?*

Yes, she thought. Yes, please.

She flicked back to Lucie's message. A hundred replies ran through her mind. None of them were right. This *situation* wasn't right. Her shining, glittering finger hovered above the screen. Not replying, pretending she hadn't yet read the message, felt as wrong as all the other potential replies—and cowardly too—but it was all she had.

She rolled onto her side, as if this time she really could roll away from the problem, and tapped once more on Scotty's name.

22

My brain is exploding, she read a few minutes—and several messages—later. *In a good way.*

That didn't make sense, but the edges of Edee's mouth had turned upwards a touch anyway. He was interested and he wasn't freaked out (as far as she could tell from words on a screen). She did not care about metaphorical accuracy. In this messed up day, she did not care about that at all.

How did it start? came his next message. *You woke up like it one day? You had a spider moment? How can I get it too?*

I got some glasses, Edee wrote, before describing in as few words as possible how she no longer needed them to see the lines and how they were everywhere.

The next moment he was calling her. His face had a strange glow from whatever light he had in his room. She didn't care about that, either.

"Which optician's?" he said.

"The little one off the high street," murmured Edee, hoping Mum was asleep. "Heliosons. The one with a black and white sign, near that cafe with the flowers outside."

"Heliosons," said Scotty. "I'm making an appointment. Do you want to come?"

It sounded so easy, so simple.

"Do you?" said Scotty.

She nodded. "I don't think you could fake the test. Do you need glasses?"

"I could tell them I'm getting headaches," said Scotty. "That's what happened to Dad before he got his."

Edee nodded, a little unconvinced. But it would be going back, and she could tell Lucie . . . no, she didn't want to think about her at the moment. He was interested. She wanted to concentrate on that.

"And even if I don't, we could ask where the lenses come from and who makes them," said Scotty. "I could try the display ones on."

"I didn't see anything through those ones," said Edee, then wished she hadn't. "But you might."

"It's worth a try," said Scotty. "And everyone's lines are different?"

"Yeah," said Edee. "Loads of people's look similar but they're always different. They're different widths and make up different patterns, and then some people's look really different. Thicker, for example." She didn't tell him about his dad.

"Like fingerprints," said Scotty.

"Yeah." It was a good comparison aside from the obvious problem. The one he didn't know about yet. "But Amber and other babies don't have any."

"Oh," said Scotty. "I see. That's what you meant about Amber. Then it isn't DNA, unless they're like second teeth or something." He looked away for a moment. "Snowflakes are meant to all be different."

She was going to have to tell him the other bit. The head bit. And she wanted to. "People make them. I've seen it happen. They start as a bead of light and then circle their body. When the ends meet it makes a line."

"I've done that?" said Scotty.

"Yeah," said Edee. "I think so."

"And I didn't know," said Scotty. He looked impressed.

Edee nodded. "I think Amber hasn't learned how to make them yet."

"And we don't know that we can," he said. "That's . . . awesome. It's evidence. If we have one power like that there must be others." His eyes shone in the same way they had earlier in the evening. "This is some epic silver lining to my mum and the Reg thing. Thanks, Edee."

He was *thanking* her? Seriously, this whole day could not get any more turned about. "I didn't ask to see it," she said. Somehow it felt important he knew that. "It kind of happened. I was . . . I mean I didn't know what was going on at first. I thought . . ."

He was nodding. "But you did. And you told me."

Why do you believe me? That's what Edee wanted to ask but she didn't. He believed her. She did not want him to change his mind.

"It makes so much sense," said Scotty. "Doesn't it? There has to be stuff going on that we don't know about. I wonder why the glasses helped you to see it. And why you don't need them now."

Edee chewed her lip. "It's like it's trying to help, whatever it is. Like it's revealing more stuff every time I understand a bit more."

Scotty nodded slowly. "Epic."

"Yeah," said Edee.

"Tell me again," said Scotty. "Describe it all. From the start."

"Okay." She felt more awake than she had for days. "It started with the eye test I suppose. They said that . . ."

THE NEXT MORNING Edee woke up late. It was after eleven when she went into the bathroom and cleaned her teeth. Mum was in her office. The wheeled chair clattered across the floorboards as Edee crossed the hallway again.

"That was a long sleep."

Edee nodded. It hadn't been really. She and Scotty had chatted until after three.

"Lucie called," said Mum.

"When?" said Edee. The sleep fog in her head disappeared. "You?"

"No, the landline," said Mum.

"The landline?"

"She said you hadn't returned a call," said Mum.

"I was asleep," said Edee.

"That's what I told her," said Mum. "And that I was sure you'd phone her as soon as you woke up."

From the look on Mum's face, Lucie hadn't said anything more. But calling the landline. It was persistent, insistent. Then again, what else should she expect from Lucie? When she—the Lucieness—was going with you it was such a good thing, so good you didn't really notice it. This didn't feel like that at all. What on earth was Edee going to say to her?

"Is everything alright?" said Mum.

"Mmm," said Edee. It sounded unconvincing, weak. She faked a yawn and began moving again. "I'll go and call her."

"There's fresh bread on the side when you want breakfast," called Mum. "And I made you another smoothie. It's in the fridge."

Edee shut her door, picked up her phone, and sat on her bed. It was still warm. Maybe Rosa and Greg had decided to climb some signal-free mountain today or return to the phone-free retreat or were insisting on a phone-free day. Please. She tapped on her number. One ring. *Please*. Two. She almost hung up.

"Finally," said Lucie.

Edee swallowed. A horrible feeling of dread was unfurling in her stomach. "Hi."

There was a pause, then Lucie said, "How are—"

While Edee said, "Have you—"

"Sorry—"

"Sorry—"

"You go," said Lucie.

Edee bit her lip. She didn't want to go first.

"Shall I?" said Lucie.

"Yeah, you."

There was a pause. Wait, Lucie didn't know what to say either? This was . . . worse than she'd thought.

"Where are you?" said Edee.

"At the campsite," said Lucie. "We're . . . Mum and Dad are chatting to the people in the van next door."

"Right," said Edee. "Good. I mean, is it good? Are they nice?" Good? Nice? This was awful.

"Yeah, they are. They're from Norway. They've got two kids and two dogs."

"Right," said Edee again. "That must be, um, a bit of a squash."

"Not really," said Lucie.

"Right," said Edee.

"Listen," said Lucie, "I'm not sure how long they're going to be, and . . ."

"And what?" said Edee, as if she couldn't guess.

"And I'm worried," said Lucie. "So are Cass and Maddie."

They'd been talking about this? About her?

146

"We think—"

"You told them?" said Edee.

"Only a bit," said Lucie. "Not much, just that you—"

"You promised." Edee's stomach pulled tight. She tried to swallow, but her throat was even tighter.

There was another pause. "They knew something was going on anyway. They said you practically ran from the house and Maddie said—"

"Because I wanted to tell you." Edee's voice cracked. She spoke a touch louder, which somehow forced it to be level. "I'd just seen their lines come back and . . ."

"Edes." Lucie's voice had lowered. "You're talking about lines, about things you're seeing. I'm worried. We want to help you."

"Then believe me," said Edee. "I'm not making it up."

"I'm sure it seems real," said Lucie. "But—"

"There's no but."

"There is."

Edee took a long, silent breath. If only Lucie would listen. "You don't understand. It's epic."

"Right," said Lucie quietly.

"Look, I'm fine," said Edee. Her voice shook again, not from anything to do with the lines but to do with this, with Lucie. "Let's not talk about it."

"I can't—"

"You can," said Edee.

"I don't think—"

"Then don't think about it."

"That's crazy," said Lucie. She was shaking her head. Edee could tell by the way the words shifted.

"This isn't going anywhere." Edee closed her eyes. "I'll call you back later. I'll try and—"

"You're," started Lucie. "It's . . . pretending it's not . . ."

Lucie never spoke like this, stilted and pausing.

"I don't want to argue," said Edee. It was a stupid thing to say. They already were.

"I'm not arguing," said Lucie. It was barely audible and then she hung up.

Edee opened her eyes. Her whole body seemed to be lit up with flickering light. So many of the lines were glowing and glittering. It had to mean something. She shook her head. How was it even possible to think about that after *that*?

———

Sunday afternoon seemed immune to Edee's mood and her dread of the week ahead and all it would bring—seeing Cass and Maddie again, the counselling appointment, some kind of weird contact with Lucie—and rolled on regardless. She managed to avoid too many questions from Mum, helped in no small part by the fact that Mum stayed in her office until after four and only emerged to say she needed to go out. For once, Edee would have been only too happy to have tagged along but, for once, Mum did not offer.

As soon as the front door closed, she headed to the lounge and slumped on the sofa, as much for a change of scenery as anything else. She lay one way then the other, wishing she felt tired, but her head was buzzing and now her phone was ringing. Almost, she stayed where she was, except ignoring it hadn't exactly worked out so well yesterday. If it was Cass or Maddie, then . . .

By the time she got to her room, the answerphone had kicked in. It was Scotty.

He picked up after one ring. "Your mum's turned up at ours—"

Edee's eyebrows raised involuntarily.

"—I figured that meant I should speak to you. Want to meet outside Melling's?"

The hesitation lasted for half a second. "Sure."

She almost texted Mum but, on second thoughts, she scribbled a note instead and left it in the kitchen.

23

S cotty was already outside the fish and chip shop. He was leaning against the wall with one knee bent, his foot against the brickwork. He raised the opposite hand in greeting.

"What's my mum doing at yours?" she asked, as soon as she was close enough for him to hear.

"Didn't stay to find out," said Scotty, holding the paper bag out towards her. There was a serving of ketchup to one side. "Talking about my mum, probably."

Edee took a chip.

"The other side's got vinegar," said Scotty.

The other side. For a split second, she thought he meant Lucie, but that was ridiculous. He didn't even know her.

Scotty pushed himself away from the wall and the two of them began walking. He held out the bag again and Edee helped herself. She didn't know if they were walking somewhere in particular. She didn't ask.

"The optician's is closed on Sundays," said Scotty. "I checked."

"Yeah," said Edee. "Mum chose it." Spending Sunday

evening with Lucie had once been so normal. This was not so different yet completely different at the same time.

"She wouldn't've expected any of this though," said Scotty.

"No," said Edee. "I mean as far as I know. But she couldn't have. It's not . . . she's not . . ."

They walked in silence for a minute or so.

"I haven't told her," said Edee.

"Yeah," said Scotty. "I get that." They walked a few more paces before he added, "What can you see now?"

She described it all as best she could, starting with his lines, then moving to her own, and then to other people who stayed around long enough for her to do a decent job of describing them. Now and then he asked a question that prompted her to go into more detail, to try and be more accurate or to find a new way to describe the same thing. It was impossible to describe it properly, of course, to convey the detail in the lines and the way the glittering was so alive, so responsive, so connected to the person within. At one point, she tried to compare the quality of the light emanating from them to the headlights on the cars going by. She soon gave up. It was nothing like that light.

He asked about the eye test again, wanting to know about it in microscopic detail. That took them back to the moment she'd first tried the glasses on; how she'd seen the light around the optician first, and had thought it had been something about him until she'd seen Mum's lines soon after. They finished the chips as they walked. Scotty threw the paper into a bin before they turned away from the busy road and on to the path by the canal.

"And there are words on the lines," he said. "And only people have them."

Neither were questions, more summaries or statements, but Edee nodded anyway.

"Nothing else?" said Scotty. "No plants or animals or anything?"

"No," said Edee. "Not that I've seen. Maybe there's another set of glasses for that."

"I don't know," said Scotty. "It seems like it's—"

"Human," finished Edee.

"Yeah," said Scotty.

They carried on in silence for a bit. The canal path, as was the nature of the thing, went on and on. Here and there they passed under a bridge. The sun had got a little lower. At some point they were going to have to turn back. Edee did not want to be the one to suggest it. After today, she would happily keep on and on.

"Listen," said Scotty suddenly. "This isn't only about the lines."

This? What this? "Walking?" said Edee. "Talking?"

"Yeah," he said. "Because it is. But it's also . . ." He was frowning, as if he was trying to work out how to say whatever it was he wanted her to know. "This might sound stupid, but . . ."

They took a few more steps. Edee already knew it wasn't going to sound stupid and, even if it did, there was no way she was going to say that to him. He'd listened to her. He was here.

"I wonder about this kind of thing all the time," said Scotty. "Not *this* obviously, but about things we don't know. Things that must be around us which we can't see, but I've never spoken to anyone who thinks there's more, you know, other stuff and . . . I like it."

Edee glanced sideways. He was looking at her too. She nodded. The thing was, she hadn't thought about anything like this until the Thursday in the optician's. Not really, not in the way he meant. She'd never known people *did*.

"I watch videos sometimes," he said. "Not about crazy

things or screwed-up stuff, they're just different. So I know people do think about them too, but I've never had these kinds of conversations with another person. Not like this."

Edee was wondering how come she'd met Scotty at exactly the right moment and how come he'd called today. All of a sudden, her brain felt like it was way, way too small. She rubbed her eyes. The point was that he was here. And he was still looking at her. It was almost shy. She would never have imagined the boy who'd been sat in the bucket chair the other day could ever be shy.

"I'm glad you think about this stuff," she said slowly, "because I didn't, and now I do and having someone else who knows about it is . . . I don't know. It helped that you believed me. It is helping."

Scotty scuffed one of the stones at the side of the path with his foot. "I don't get why anyone wouldn't. But they won't. My mum wouldn't. Neither would my dad. They'd pretend a bit. They used to do that when I was little. I'd ask them questions and they'd make up some stupid answer, like I'd be satisfied with that. I used to think they just didn't know the answers, which they didn't, but then I realised they didn't get the questions either. They wouldn't even consider them."

"What sort of questions?"

Scotty kicked the stone again. It bumped along the earthy path and back into the undergrowth. "Things like how could you tell if someone was from the future? I asked Dad that once and he told me I'd been watching too many films. But it's a good question because if time travel is possible one day, then people from the future must be here, unless you can only travel back to the point it began or something." They moved to the side of the path as a couple of cyclists headed towards them. "And then there's the thing about the world turning, that it's turning under our feet—it's moving while we're on it—but we have no idea. We can't feel it. All we've got is the way the sky changes, the stars, and hardly anyone notices that either."

The cyclists went past giving brief, businesslike nods.

"I asked Mum about that," continued Scotty. "And she said 'why do we need to know?' But that wasn't the point." He ran his hand along the top of the grass that grew alongside the path. "Once Mum was complaining about the noise the birds were making in the garden. And I said they might be having a conversation. She said 'they're birds Scotty, not people.' But I thought we don't know they aren't talking. I still think that. So many people assume we're more sophisticated than other animals. But birds get around the world with nothing: no luggage, no map, no water bottles. They know stuff we've no idea about."

Edee didn't know what to say. The world already looked so different from the way it had looked a few weeks ago, and all of a sudden it felt like it had expanded in a whole other way too. Something, a bat perhaps, darted in front of them, silhouetted against the darkening world. "It should've been you who saw the lines."

"I wish it had been," said Scotty. "But I'll take knowing about it for now because the things you're seeing proves we don't know anything. It's . . ."

"Epic," said Edee.

"Yeah," said Scotty. "And not."

Exactly. That was exactly how she'd felt in the cafe with Kitty and later, too—that somehow it all made perfect sense.

"They're not interested in this," said Scotty after a moment. "But they'll go on at each other for hours about whose fault it is that Mum met Reg and whether Amber should go to nursery every day. I don't get it."

"Yeah," said Edee. Just like she couldn't get Lucie not being interested in this.

"How was Scotty?" said Mum.

"Good." Edee had only just got back. Mum had been coming out of the bathroom. Edee had headed to the kitchen, trying to act like this was some regular Sunday evening.

Mum had followed her. She'd opened the fridge as if she'd meant to come in here but she wasn't taking anything from it. "What did you do?"

"Got some chips." Edee picked up a glass and turned on the tap. "Walked for a bit."

"Walked?"

"Yeah."

"Right," said Mum. "Did you talk?"

"Yeah."

There was a pause before Mum said, "Good."

Edee turned the tap off and took a sip of water before taking a couple of steps towards the door. Mum's lines were glittering. So were her own. The image she'd had before, of the lines playing a tune she could not hear, came back. If that were true, would hers and Mum's complement each other or would they clash? What about hers and Scotty's? Hers and Lucie's?

"And he's alright?" said Mum, as if asking the same thing in a different way might get a different response.

"Yes." Edee was suddenly aware of the glass in her hand again.

"Was it just the two of you?"

"Yeah."

A couple more lines over Mum shone. She shut the

fridge door, picked up the kettle, and moved to the sink. "Would you like a tea?"

"No thanks," said Edee. "I'm going to go to bed."

Mum glanced towards the window and then towards the clock. "Did he walk you back?"

"Yes."

"Good," said Mum. "I'm glad you saw him. I saw Craig, as you probably know."

This time Edee didn't say anything.

"Amber's such a delight," said Mum. "I don't understand how Jo could leave her. Any of them. I'm glad you saw Scotty, I really am."

Edee was too, yet for totally different reasons, ones she would not have been able to explain even if she'd wanted to. The obvious part—the glaringly obvious part—was that Scotty had helped her more than the other way around, but she wasn't going to say that either. Luckily, Mum was staring at the jars of teabags like they were the most fascinating things ever. She did not seem to notice her daughter leaving the room.

24

The next morning, Edee walked to school again. She slowed when she got to the park and wandered through it with little awareness or interest in the time. It wasn't that she was trying to put off seeing Cass and Maddie, well, that too, but there was something else, something bigger. It was . . . school itself seemed so much smaller now. All of those things she and Scotty had spoken about last night, they weren't covered in the subjects they sat through day after day. Or rather, she couldn't remember them being there and surely she would? Scotty certainly didn't and he would have noticed for sure. And even if they were, where would they fit? Physics? Biology? RE? English? Maths? All of them? Or in a completely different, new subject? Perhaps it didn't fit in school at all. That seemed right. It was too big, too uncontainable.

She looked out at the light radiating from the runners, the walkers, the commuters, the people, all around her. If Scotty had got the glasses and had walked through this park or another one, he wouldn't have been freaked out by it, his heart wouldn't have thumped in terror, he wouldn't have ripped them from his face. He would have been interested, and curious, and probably regretful that he didn't have anyone to talk to about it. But now he did and so did she. In some ways that was as unbelievable as seeing the lines in the first place.

Certainty flooded through her veins as she moved through the park and the background blurred to her awareness again. She was going to get better at describing all of this so that he would be able to picture it in photographic quality for himself. And she would try and edit a photo after all. It would be worth it if it helped him to visualise the magnitude of this thing. The thing he'd accepted so simply. He hadn't tried to pull it all apart to try and figure out what it was; he'd been interested because of what it suggested rather than what it was. Really, that was just as interesting.

Fifteen minutes or so later, something bumped against her arm. She jumped, her attention reluctantly leaving behind pictures and epic and last night, and becoming aware of the path around her, the school gates up ahead, and of Cass, who had appeared by her side, and Maddie who was a little bit further away, listening.

"What's going on?" said Cass.

"Huh?" said Edee.

"Huh?" repeated Cass. Her tone was a little bit playful and a little bit dramatic. She began speaking as if from a list. "Saturday morning happened, then you ran away from us like we were infectious. In the afternoon you weren't where you said you were going to be, then you turned invisible. We've been waving at you for the last five minutes, and now you're saying 'huh?' like we're being unreasonable."

"I . . ." began Edee.

"Is there anything you want to tell us?" Cass nudged her arm again.

Edee turned her face from the intense glittering at her

side and focused on the dull, grey tarmac. It didn't help. Her own lines were illuminating that space. She didn't want to tell them about it all, not right now. But Lucie already had. If she didn't say anything, everything would only get more difficult and she didn't want difficult. She wanted to be where she'd been a few minutes ago.

Cass, however, was fidgeting and Edee knew she had to reply. She took one, two more steps then opened her mouth wishing she knew what to say. "It's . . ." She stuttered, stopped, and started again. The truth, that's what she'd give them. "Since I got my glasses I've been able to see this stuff and—"

"Yeah, we know that," said Cass. "Lucie said. They're adding stripes to everything, although I didn't see any when I had them on. Anything else?"

The rest of the cutoff sentence felt like it was trailing from her mouth. Anything else? Yes. There was a whole other part of the world—*parts*—that they had no idea about and—

"Anything about yesterday, for instance?" said Cass.

Yesterday? Did she mean Saturday? In the supermarket? Or had Lucie told them everything about their phone call? Or—

"Yesterday evening to be precise," said Cass. "You and a boy. Six o'clock."

It felt like the path had dropped away beneath her feet. What? How could she possibly know that?

"Walking down Station Road," said Cass. "Eating chips. That was you, right?"

"I . . . yes," said Edee. "How—"

"We had Thai for dinner," said Cass. "Mum and I drove past you and some boy, deep in conversation. Who is he? When were you going to tell us?"

They'd reached the main school building and Edee,

gratefully, let herself be jostled by the crowd making their way inside. It did not last long. At the top of the stairs, Cass came alongside her once more. Maddie was there too. She still hadn't said anything.

"Who is he?" said Cass again. "Why's he a secret? I've told you everything about Ty."

If this had been an ordinary day, Maddie would have made some comment about that. She didn't. Her lips were flat.

"He's a friend." Edee's face was burning. She could feel sweat above her lip. No. They were going to think she was embarrassed. They'd make so much more of it, get the wrong idea. He was a friend, that was all, but their conversation, *that* conversation, Cass and Maddie wouldn't get it. They were going to—

"From where?" said Cass. "How do you know him."

"From ages ago," muttered Edee. "My mum knows his dad. I hadn't seen him for ages."

"What, and you bumped into him in the chip shop?" said Cass. "And the chips flew into your mouth?" There was a complicated edge to her voice now, part interest, part sarcasm, and perhaps part disbelief that Edee could know someone she did not.

"No," said Edee. "We met there." She could say about Scotty's parents, but she didn't want to. "It wasn't planned, only a few minutes before. We were talking."

"About what?" said Cass. "Us?"

"No," said Edee. "About—"

"Lucie?" said Cass.

"No," said Edee. "None of you. We were talking about . . ." How could she even describe it? "Life stuff."

"Life stuff?" Cass looked towards Maddie, who shrugged. They'd reached their form room and automatically headed to the seats in the third row.

"Is there something wrong?" said Maddie. She spoke quietly, confidentially, like something in the vicinity was breakable. "Lucie said that—"

"No," said Edee. "She thinks . . . there's nothing wrong. It's the opposite." It was so hard to explain. Scotty had just *known*. It had been so easy. This . . . was not.

"The opposite?" said Cass. "Everything's wrong?"

"No," said Edee, pushing on with the truth. This truth. "It's right. I meant right."

"How can not telling us things and Lucie saying that . . . how can it be right?" said Maddie.

Cass was leaning forward on her chair as she did so often. "Do you mean the boy? With the boy?"

"Morning," said Mr Lewin, as he entered the room and sat on his chair.

Edee lowered her head, for once happy to see him, yet also feeling that Cass and Maddie had joined in on the surveillance. Lucie too. Her phone vibrated against her foot. Reflexively, she reached down to lift her whole bag onto her lap. There was enough noise and movement in the classroom for Mr Lewin not to notice and, anyway, the bell hadn't gone yet, not quite. It was something to do, something to occupy her hands and eyes, and Cass and Maddie would think it was normal. They'd probably think it was Lucie. It wasn't. For once, Edee did not dwell on that.

Optician's later, coming? Half three?

Yes, replied Edee, *meet you there*.

She let the bag slide back to the floor. Cass was also texting. Maddie was looking straight ahead, a concerned, confused look on her face.

For the rest of the day, Edee tried to carry on as if everything was normal—or as normal as it had been since Lucie had left. Even so, every now and then she caught Cass or Maddie looking at her or the two of them sharing a glance or a whisper. Luckily (she'd never thought of it as lucky before) she had the last two classes apart from them on Monday afternoons.

As soon as the final bell began, Edee scooped her belongings into her bag, muttered a quick "see you later" to no one in particular, and was first to the bus stop. Within fifteen minutes she was propped up on the low wall a little along from the optician's, watching the people and lines going by. She was back to thinking about a picture. How could she show the animate sense of them in something that did not move? Maybe it would have to be a video. If only she could get Maddie to help. She shook her head. She didn't want to think about her or any of them right now.

"Hey."

"Hi."

Scotty had his hands in his pockets, the strap from his school bag was slung across his chest. He was smiling. "They said you had to have a parent come and sign some forms if you want a test. I thought we should go in anyway and ask a few questions. Dad picks Amber up after work. He'd need weeks of notice."

"Okay." Edee moved towards him. She wondered about his mum, but did not ask.

The two of them made their way along the path and into the optician's. The receptionist—the same one who'd been working when Edee had been in for her eye test—was on the phone. She had the handset tucked between her ear and shoulder and was tapping a screen at the same time. A bell had rung when they'd entered the shop. She had not looked up.

Scotty scanned the rows of frames. "Those are yours?" he murmured, indicating the stand in the far corner.

"Yeah," said Edee. "You don't need an eye test."

He laughed.

"This place is so normal," said Edee. It was more than strange to think it had been there, just to the right, that she had first seen the lines. It might have been months ago, not a matter of days.

"Brilliantly normal," said Scotty.

"Yes," said the receptionist. "Nine tomorrow . . . yes, of course . . . okay, yes, bring it with you . . . thanks very much." She put the phone down and scribbled on a piece of paper. "Hello. How can I help?" She tapped the screen again. "Have you got an appointment?"

"No," said Scotty. "We've got some questions."

She nodded, adding something to the note.

"About astronomy."

Edee almost said, "What?"

The receptionist looked up.

Scotty smiled.

The receptionist did not smile but she did give a sort of respectful nod. "Go ahead."

"I want to book an eye test," said Scotty. "I know my dad needs to sign the forms, but he works late."

"We're open on Saturday mornings," said the receptionist. "Could he make a weekend?"

"Maybe," said Scotty. "He's a bit busy at the moment."

"Are you experiencing any problems with your eyesight?"

Scotty shook his head. "No. My friend got some glasses and I thought I should get mine checked."

"Very sensible," said the receptionist. "When was the last time you had them tested?"

"I don't know," said Scotty. "I can't remember."

"In that case, it sounds like you're due one. Have you been here before?"

"No," said Scotty. "But there were some frames I liked."

He twisted his body towards the side of the shop with the display that held the twin to Edee's.

"We can order others in," said the receptionist. She picked up a couple of leaflets and fanned them out on the counter. "This one explains all the benefits of eye tests for young people and this one covers the prices and the services you're entitled to. Perhaps with notice he'd be able to accompany you, once he realises how important regular eye tests are?"

Scotty took them.

"It really is important," said the receptionist. "Eyesight is a gift."

Edee's eyes widened. The optician had said that.

"How old are you?"

"Fifteen," said Scotty.

The receptionist nodded. "Our phone number is on the back if he has any questions. Someone else could also accompany you. Another family member, for example."

"Yeah," said Scotty. "How do they work?"

"There's nothing to worry about," said the receptionist. "In fact, some people your age find the equipment quite interesting."

"I meant the glasses," said Scotty. "The lenses. How do they make people see properly?"

"Oh." She sat back. "The science is not my department, I'm afraid. I work with clients, rather than the glasses themselves. One of the optometrists would be able to explain it to you. It's to do with the way the light reflects on to the eye, that's as much as I know."

"Right," said Scotty. "Light being refracted, that sort of thing?"

"There's a poster over there." She pointed to a noticeboard on the wall between the two consulting rooms. "If you've time to wait, Marsha would be able to answer those kinds of questions. She'll be finished in twenty minutes or so. You could also ask during the eye test, of course."

"Great," said Scotty. "Is the man here? Could I ask him?"

"The man?" said the receptionist, frowning.

Scotty turned towards Edee. "Yeah, the man."

The scene from last time was running through Edee's mind. He'd told her his name. He'd said the thing about clarity of vision and then he'd said . . . "Jonathan."

The receptionist shook her head. "There's no one here called Jonathan."

"Yes there is," said Edee. "I got my glasses from here a couple of weeks ago and he fitted them."

"You must be mistaken," said the receptionist. "It was a different practice, I expect. There are a few who attempt to imitate us."

Edee pointed to the seat that was just visible behind the counter. "I sat there, and he altered them at that machine. He was called Jonathan. He told me."

The woman gave an appeasing sort of smile and switched her attention back to Scotty. "Any other questions?"

Edee slipped one shoulder from her bag and moments later held up the glasses case. "Look, he gave me this." The white Helioson's logo in its elaborate font was scrawled across the fabric. "It was definitely here."

"That's an old case," said the receptionist. "We haven't used those for months now."

"You were here," said Edee, "when I had my eyes tested. It was only a few weeks ago. I had two appointments. You could check. I'll be on record. The second was with Jonathan."

The receptionist straightened the row of already straight leaflets. She could not have made it more obvious that she had no intention of checking anything and that she thought Edee was exceptionally slow. "I've worked here for twelve years and I can assure you there has never been anyone employed here who has gone by the name Jonathan." Once again, her attention moved to Scotty. Edee might as well have been see-through.

"He gave me a card," she muttered, and scrabbled in her bag again.

"Jon?" said Scotty. "Jonny? J?"

The receptionist shook her head.

There was a silence.

"Can I try a few pairs on?" said Scotty.

"Of course. Our men's range and the unisex frames are to the left. If you take any photos, please make sure there are no other clients in the background. If you do find some frames elsewhere that you like we can usually order them in, as I said."

Scotty glanced around. There was no one else in the shop. He smiled and moved away.

Edee, one hand still in her bag, followed. "I'm not making it up," she whispered.

"I know," said Scotty.

"She wasn't even here when I picked up the glasses. No one was. He said he was multitasking. She's wrong."

"Probably," said Scotty, unhooking the frames he'd pointed at earlier and putting them on. He spoke in an even lower tone. "But what if she's not? What if you're both right?" He raised and lowered his head peering under, through, then above the frames. "Just saying."

"You mean—"

"A mysterious non-existent Jonathan thrown into the mix," said Scotty. "Why not?"

25

W hen Edee got home, she took everything out of her bag, but the optician's card was simply not there. She held the bag upside down and shook it before putting everything back in, one item at a time. There was nothing that even resembled a card. There wasn't even any paper. She scanned her room but was certain she had not taken it out. Maggie's card was over there on her desk. It had been in her blazer pocket and she'd taken it out in case someone had seen. But the other one had definitely been in her bag. Which meant . . . it couldn't mean what it seemed to mean, could it?

She opened her laptop and typed 'invisible people' and then 'invisibility', and 'can someone be invisible'. However, just as it had been on the evening she'd got the glasses, the internet was no help at all.

He couldn't be invisible. It just wasn't possible. Except, until a couple of weeks ago she wouldn't have ever thought that light emanating from people would've been possible either. What if Scotty was right about him? What if there was way, way more going on around them that, ordinarily, they had no idea about? What if the lines and the birds really were the tip of some strange iceberg?

A strange iceberg that wasn't all that strange. Once again, she couldn't help but think about the moments when something to do with the lines had felt so right. How was it possible for something so odd to feel so right? It was impossible to ignore, that was for sure, even if she had no idea what to do with it.

And she couldn't ignore Lucie for much longer, either. There had been no messages all day and the weight of that wrong finally descended on her. It was as if a hole had ripped open in her world. She turned her phone off and on again, just in case something somewhere had got jammed, but nothing flashed up. Even the group chats were silent. She tapped on Lucie's name and stared at the keyboard for five, ten minutes. But Lucie had been the one who hadn't listened and, if she didn't want to talk to her, Edee wouldn't force it.

Her eyes tingled. Three weeks, that was all it had taken for them to have a day without speaking when they could. And she had so much to say. She wanted to tell her about the receptionist and the potentially invisible man. Why had one part of her life turned upside down just as another had become so interesting? It was terrible, terrible timing.

There was a knock on her door. She swiped her fingers across her eyes.

"Dinner will be ready in five minutes," said Mum. "And I've rearranged an appointment tomorrow afternoon so I can drop you at counselling."

"Okay," said Edee. A silent, ironic laugh jammed into the lump in her throat.

"It's so nice to see you again." Maggie was sitting in the same chair and had assumed the same position as last week, legs tucked back and hands clasped. The lines covering her were glittering in a similar way too. "How has your week been?"

"Fine," said Edee. The room was also indistinguishable from eight days before, even the cards were identically placed. In fact, the only thing that looked different at all was the box of tissues on the table. It was less full.

"Is there anything you'd like us to begin with today?" said the counsellor. There was a pause, then she added, "It could be anything. It doesn't matter how small."

Edee watched the tissue box. She wondered who else had sat in this chair since she'd been here, what they'd spoken about, and whether any of them could possibly have had a week to match her own.

"Why don't you start by telling me a little about what's happened since we last saw each other? Perhaps something you've done or simply something that occurs to you?"

The middle of Edee's eyebrows raised a fraction. She imagined telling the woman every single thing from the last week, step by curious step, until they reached today and the weird pleasantness that Maddie and Cass had assumed each time they'd been around her. Neither of them had mentioned the lack of messages, so Edee hadn't either. It had hung, unspoken, between them all day.

"I always find it interesting to hear what my clients get up to day-to-day," said Maggie. "I've learned about all sorts over the years. Fishing, painting, yoga, carpentry, you name it."

Lights? Lines? Edee doubted it somehow. Her mouth remained shut.

"Okay," said Maggie, after an even longer pause.

"That's okay. Let's see. Have you heard from your friend this week? It's Lucie, isn't it?"

Edee nodded. Her throat tightened. She forced herself to think about how odd it was that Lucie's absence was such a massive part of her world, yet the counsellor had only just about remembered her name.

"Have you heard from her?" prompted Maggie.

Edee's stomach twisted. She nodded for a second time.

"Is it all messages?" said Maggie. "Have you spoken?"

It was exactly the same as last time, impossible to keep quiet when questions were flowing in only one direction. "Yeah. We've spoken." There was another pause. This time Maggie didn't fill it and, because it was easier and true, Edee found herself saying, "I stayed at another friend's on Friday. She was there online."

"Online?"

"On the screen."

"Oh," said Maggie. "I see. And how was that?"

Edee's stomach twisted tighter. Did it count as lying if the thing you said was half true? "It was good. Different and stuff, but it was good to see her."

"The other friend knows her too?" said Maggie.

"Yeah. There were four of us. Before." Somehow she managed to keep her voice level.

"I see," said Maggie again. "You and Lucie and two others?"

"Yeah."

"Was the fourth person there, too, the other evening?"

Edee nodded.

"How did you feel, seeing Lucie on the screen?" said Maggie.

Edee moved her shoulders in a tiny shrug. "It was good." There was another silence, a longer one. She remembered the thing she'd said to Mum and found herself saying it again, "But there's always someone else around now. Either her mum and dad or people here. It's not the same."

Maggie nodded slowly. "You've had a lot of change."

And she didn't know half of it.

"Would you say you've experienced a lot of change before this?" said Maggie.

Edee shook her head.

"It can be very challenging," said Maggie. "Change is something many people find difficult. I have lots of conversations about it with clients of all ages."

Edee glanced at the tissue box again.

"What sort of things did you want to speak to her about?" said Maggie. "Would it be helpful to talk to me about any of them?"

The twists in Edee's belly were joined by the old ache of Lucie's physical absence and the newer discomfort of the lingering silence. Her eyes tingled. No. Whatever else happened she was not going to cry. She tried to think about Scotty and the canal.

"It's alright," said Maggie. "I realise I'm no substitute for someone your own age and neither would I pretend to be, but I want to reiterate that this space and time is for you. We can talk about anything you would like to. Nothing is off the table, so to speak."

Edee wished the clock was not angled away from her.

"Okay," said Maggie. "Let's see. Could you tell me what life was like before Lucie went away?"

Edee could and she did, because that, at least, was easy, even if the twists tightened and multiplied as she spoke.

The description led to more questions from Maggie, asking her to describe the ways in which life felt different now, and how Cass and Maddie were similar to Lucie and different to her, and how Lucie had been when they'd spoken. Edee's voice caught once or twice. Each time she swallowed and swallowed, and somehow managed to keep going.

Eventually there was yet another pause. This time it was broken by Maggie saying, "Edee, I'm curious, if you could wave a magic wand—

It was such a surprising question that Edee found herself meeting the woman's eyes properly for the first time. Magic?

"—what would you change?"

"Um." Edee chewed her lip.

"I'm asking because sometimes thinking about a situation from a different perspective can be helpful. Enlightening, so to speak."

Magic? Enlightening? The lines over the woman's body were glittering as much as they had been since the two of them had sat down, perhaps a little more. "You mean . . ."

"I mean that sometimes looking at a situation from different angles, different sides, is helpful. And sometimes it can help us find the first practical step towards making a change or recognising a change in ourselves. For example, if you had a magic wand, would you bring Lucie here right now?"

Edee sank. It was just a coincidence. A couple of words. And once upon a time, a few days ago, that question would have been such a simple one to answer, but now . . . if Lucie hadn't gone, would that have meant she wouldn't have seen the lines or had those conversations with Scotty? Would she erase those things? And yet, everything had been so much simpler before. It had been two and two making four. Equal. Reliable.

Except hadn't the lines always been there, just invisible?

"I don't know. Sometimes I would and sometimes I

wouldn't, because . . ." She looked down at her glittering body then at the glittering opposite.

"Because what?" asked Maggie. "Can you tell me what's running through your mind?"

"Because . . ." There were so many things Edee could say and none she wanted to. There was one thing, however, that seemed the safest. It was also true, however much it hurt. "She's having a good time."

There was the briefest nod and smile from Maggie. Had Edee blinked at a different moment she would have missed them both. As it was, she felt like she'd passed some unknown test. A new flicker of confusion rose up alongside another of irritation. This was a strange conversation. More than that, it wasn't the one she wanted to be having. She thought of the lines again and of Scotty and heard herself saying, "Do you think there's stuff going on in the world that we can't see?"

"I'm sorry," said Maggie. "I didn't quite catch that. What did you say?"

Edee felt like she was grabbing at footholds on some invisible, sheer cliff face. "I mean, um, do you think people are more similar or more different?"

Maggie had leaned forward. She relaxed back into the chair and took a moment or two to reply. "Similar or different to who, Edee? Or what?"

"To each other."

Again, Maggie took a moment before she spoke. "That's an interesting question. What do you think?"

"I don't know," said Edee. "That's why I'm asking."

"Well." Maggie's face was back to being impassive and her tone as level as it always was. "I speak to many people, as you can imagine, and sometimes there are things that are similar between them and sometimes they are different. Everyone's circumstances are unique, of course, and there are hundreds, if not thousands, of reasons that bring us together. But I do see patterns as well, sometimes. It's hard to say. I think there are many, many factors to our experience and to our situations. We're complex, all of us."

"But if you had to pick one," pressed Edee, "which would you choose, similar or different?"

"Why would we have to choose?" said Maggie. "I'm curious, Edee. Do you think it's one or the other? Could there be a third option?"

But similar and different were opposites. How could the answer be something else? It didn't make sense. Then again, everyone (almost) was covered in lines, but the lines all looked different. That was similar and different.

"Perhaps it's worth considering," said Maggie. "Because lots of things in life involve grey, rather than black and white. Our circumstances can so often be testing and every person faces challenges in their life. There's no right or wrong way to face them. Sometimes we need help and the bravest thing we can do is ask for it. Like you coming to see me, Edee. I consider that to be brave above everything else."

Except she hadn't chosen. And black and white was one thing, but what about light? Where did that fit in?

"I'm pleased you asked," said Maggie. She nodded slowly. "That's exactly the kind of thing we can talk about in our time together."

Edee forced herself to smile.

26

When Maggie shepherded her back into the reception area a few minutes later, the only person Edee saw was Ruby. An hour ago, Mum had been sitting on the same chair she'd used the week before. She glanced towards the toilet. The door to it was standing open.

"Message from your mum," said Ruby. "She had to go out to an unexpected client meeting. She left you some money for the bus or said to call her and she'll pick you up as soon as she's finished."

"Okay." Edee moved forward and picked up the envelope Ruby had pointed towards. It was on top of one of Mum's business cards.

"You're welcome to wait here," said Maggie.

"It's okay," said Edee. "I get the bus all the time." She wasn't going to get the bus.

"Your mum booked your appointment for next week," said Ruby. "Everything's up together."

"You've got my number and the office number, haven't

you?" said Maggie. "If you get stuck at all, please do call us."

"Thanks." Edee slung her bag on her back and headed towards the door.

"I look forward to seeing you next week," said Maggie.

The air outside was cooler than Edee expected. She pushed her hands into her blazer pockets and turned left and left again. Her mind was full of similar, different, black, white, and grey.

Except out here in the cool air, everyone was covered, illuminated, by the glittering, sparkling light and it was neither black nor grey nor, in fact, white. Not really. It shone, that was the thing about it. That was the thing you noticed—she'd noticed—about it above everything else. A close second to that came the movement, the way the light was hardly ever constant. It was like water, in the way the sea was always moving or the way a river rippled in a breeze or dimpled with raindrops.

As she walked, her eyes un-focused and the strips of light merged into one. She imagined she was a drop in the middle of the water. A drop in an ocean. Were oceans made up of drops? Where did one drop end and the next begin? Because maybe that was the point, the fluidity. And, like this, with her eyes unfocused, the light looked like an enormous sea, even though she knew it was coming from a hundred, a thousand different places. Fluidity was not grey.

"Hello again."

Edee found herself back on the pavement. She blinked. The hello had been close, as if it had been directed towards her. It was Kitty.

"Hi," said Edee. *Kitty*. She glanced away and then back.

"You looked like you were miles away. Are you alright?"

"Yeah," said Edee. "Thanks. I'm . . . how come you're here?"

Kitty pointed down the road towards the Italian and smiled, "Commuting."

The lines covering her were as faint as before, although the pattern might have been a bit different. How curious they'd bumped into each other again. Edee almost said as much but Kitty was half a step ahead now, moving with a steady stride, and instead she found herself saying, "How come you remembered me?"

The older girl turned back. She looked surprised. "How? Well, I saw you twice. We spoke." She tipped her head to the side. "Actually, I have no idea how memory works. But you remembered me too."

Well, yes, but that was obvious. Kitty was distinctive. It would be harder not to remember her.

"Perhaps we were supposed to remember each other." Kitty's eyes shone, even though her smile had faded. She'd slowed and they were side by side again. "Hey, what happened about the job? Has your friend heard anything yet?"

"I don't think so." Edee's stomach went into a familiar twist. She'd forgotten about all that and Cass hadn't said. But then, with everything being so weird, Cass might not have told her anyway. "She met someone when we came in, one of the waiters. She's spoken about him more than the job."

"Oh," said Kitty. "Ty? That makes sense. He said he'd met someone. I didn't realise it was your friend."

"Yeah." Edee could have said more, but she didn't because thinking about Cass meant thinking about Lucie and Maddie and everything else and she didn't want to. It hurt. Everything about that hurt. Instead, she said, "How come you're talking to me?"

Kitty smiled again. "Why wouldn't I?"

"You're older," said Edee. "Older girls don't usually speak to us. At school they don't."

"Do you speak to them?" said Kitty.

"No."

Kitty laughed. "I'm kidding. I remember school. It's not that long ago." She shrugged. "I like chatting." They moved past the next shop. The lights had just gone off and someone was locking the door. "How come you're talking to me?"

Edee glanced over again.

"Still kidding," said Kitty. The faint lines around her danced. "You know, I've never wondered about memory before."

Edee hadn't either, just like she'd never wondered about other things that might be around her but not visible or audible. How come it had never occurred to her to think about those things? How come it had to Scotty? She found herself saying, "What do you think about?"

"When?" said Kitty.

"Whenever," said Edee. "Now. All the time."

"Oh," said Kitty. "I don't know. Everything? Nothing? Right now, I'm thinking about tiny memories as photos on one of those card rotators, like they have in old films. You know in offices, before there were computers." She mimed the flicking movement and laughed. "It would've been so much fun to work back then."

They walked on in silence for a few steps, then Edee said, "I didn't realise people think about different things."

"Huh," said Kitty.

"It's not like I thought everyone thought the same stuff," said Edee. "It was . . . I don't know, I didn't know some people think about stuff I'd never even thought to think about."

Kitty didn't say anything.

"Have you ever thought about that?" said Edee.

"Not really."

That was strange because she'd said about people being similar so she must've thought about it before.

"Maybe I will now." Kitty's voice rose in amusement. "When I'm not thinking about Polaroids on a roll, that is. But I probably won't. It sounds too much like being back at uni."

"You left," said Edee.

"I did," said Kitty.

"Because you didn't like thinking about stuff?"

"Because I wasn't enjoying it," said Kitty. "Some people do. I didn't."

"People are different," muttered Edee.

Kitty shifted the cotton bag she was carrying to the other hand and said, "Different and the same."

What? Wait. Back in the cafe, she'd definitely said people were the same. "How can they be both?"

"We," said Kitty.

Edee barely heard. The evidence was there, right next to her. Kitty was different. The proof was here. *There*. A few centimetres away, those faint lines. She opened her mouth to say that—to say something—but a squirrel darted across the path and scampered up one of the thin tree trunks that edged the pavement. She jumped and the words were lost.

"Imagine being able to do that," said Kitty.

Edee's eyes widened. It might have been something Scotty would have said. But that was confusing because Scotty and Kitty were definitely different. And both of them were different to Lucie. She almost stumbled on the flat path. Lucie again. She wished someone else could reach into her head and extract that particular photo for a bit or, better, that she could do it herself. She'd roll it up, shove it in a bottle, and put the lid on tight.

"Have you had dinner?" said Kitty.

"No," said Edee.

"Me neither," said Kitty. "We get free food at work. I'm going to have lasagne tonight. It smells as good as the risotto. Maybe even better."

Edee scuffed a foot along the pavement. "What do you do about things you don't want to think about?"

"Think about lasagne instead?" Kitty laughed. "I don't know. Depends why I don't want to think about it, I suppose. Fix it if it's fixable or distract myself if it isn't. So actually, yeah, lasagne." She slowed down. They'd reached the restaurant. She closed her eyes and took a long inhale. "I'm pretty sure I can smell it now. Can you?"

Edee shook her head. "Maybe."

The older girl opened her eyes. "Edes. That's what your friend called you, right?"

"Yeah."

"I'm Kitty." She raised a hand as she moved off. "Good to bump into you again." Someone was holding the door open for her and she stopped to ask how their day had been. The faint lines around her glittered. And then she was gone.

Edee, walking again, found herself thinking of Craig once more and the thick lines covering his body. And Amber and her no lines. Kitty was most like Amber and yet she was nothing like her as well. Perhaps Kitty was in her own category . . . but with the people from the photos at Maddie's? Well, no, that didn't exactly fit either. Similar and different.

Absentmindedly, she pulled her phone from her bag. There was a message from Mum asking if she wanted picking up but still nothing from Lucie.

Lucie.

Maggie, Kitty, Scotty, her own dinner, tomorrow at school, Cass and Ty, Cass and Maddie. She tried each one as a distraction, but behind them all stood Lucie. Old-Lucie. Real-Lucie.

Was it fixable?

She replied to Mum then opened a new message. Her fingers hovered for a second or two: *Hey, you okay?*

The reply came pretty quickly. It was accompanied by a photo of a table covered in food. *Yeah*, said Lucie. *Eating pizza, yum*. Minutes later, she sent the same picture to the group and Cass and Maddie both joined in too.

There was no mention of the silence. Edee's stomach gripped.

27

Over the next few weeks things settled into the shifted, newest version of new-normal. Lucie messaged the group several times a day; Edee, Cass, and Maddie hung out at school and sometimes at the weekends; and the four of them shared regular phone calls.

It was consistent but it was off, as if the world had tilted to a new angle and had jammed there. So many things nagged at Edee, like the way they had the same kinds of conversations—travelling, jobs, school, Ty, Lucie's new acquaintances, and so on—but it was as if the other three were on a slightly different time track, or that the words they used to use had acquired some new meanings which had passed Edee by. Often, she felt like she'd joined the conversation a fraction too late or that she'd forgotten something important. In fact, she spent much of the time feeling as if she had a fistful of invisible balloon strings and that she had to go about her day with them in tow, holding more tightly every time one began to drift. She wondered if someone, somewhere, might have glasses that would make the strings visible. She wondered, more than once, if that person could be Kitty, but however often she walked the road to the cafe, chance did not bring them together again.

She and Scotty messaged most days. Sometimes he'd come up with a new theory about the lines or the possibly invisible optician. Other times, they'd chat about new things one or other of them had thought about. Now and then he'd make reference to his parents' newest argument (the latest incarnation of the old argument). Once, he sent her a photo of the two of them mid-fight. He asked her what their lines were like, and she described them as best she could while not quite telling him the way they both looked like they were imprisoned. Amber was in the edge of the picture and Edee, so glad there were screens between the two of them, had found her eyes watering. That evening, she'd tried again to create a picture for him but, as ever, everything she tried seemed way, way too dull.

As the weeks went by, so did the sessions with Maggie. Mum was happy about that at least. Edee had taken to turning up with a subject to talk about. It didn't seem to matter what the starting point was, they always landed up at different or the same. Edee couldn't figure out if Maggie didn't notice or if she was simply happy they were talking. The room itself never, ever changed. Had she wanted to (she didn't), Edee could've recreated that place in every minute detail.

Whatever she was imagining though or whomever else she was talking to, the Lucie thing was never far away. Sometimes she found herself daydreaming about those long-ago times when they'd messaged each other and no one else. Now and then she tried to do so again and, although Lucie usually messaged back, she always found a reason to switch to the group chat. Calls, however, were never returned. Calls in this slanted new-normal were always four-way. Edee kept finding new reasons to leave them early.

"I get it," said Scotty.

It was the Wednesday evening before half term and Craig had invited Edee and her mum over for dinner. They were having burgers. Mum, Craig, and Amber were eating in the kitchen. Edee and Scotty had brought theirs into the lounge.

"What?" Edee put her glass on the floor and balanced the plate on her lap.

"Lucie. That's who you were talking about ages ago."

"When?" said Edee. A shiver ran through her. She'd never spoken about Lucie to him. At first she hadn't wanted to, then they were always too busy talking about other things, and then, well, she just hadn't. Mum, however, had just mentioned her (or rather mostly Rosa and Greg) in agreement with Craig that some people did, indeed, act without any regard to consequences.

"When you first said about superpowers you said you'd want someone to believe you. You meant her. That's right, isn't it?"

"Yeah," murmured Edee.

"She sounds mad," said Scotty. "Not literally. Well, maybe, but ordinary mad. As mad as most people."

"She's not mad," said Edee, stirring a chip around the pool of ketchup on her plate. Lucie was a perfectly rational, ordinary human being and that made it worse.

"But she didn't believe you?" said Scotty.

"No," said Edee. "She still doesn't." Not that she knew for sure, of course. They still hadn't spoken about it since that awful phone call. It seemed a pretty safe assumption.

"She's missing out," said Scotty, around a mouthful of burger.

"She's in Slovenia," said Edee. "Cass thinks she's got it all."

"Who's Cass?" said Scotty.

"Someone else," said Edee. "My friend who wants to go travelling." She wished Mum hadn't mentioned Lucie. She did not want that world spilling into this one.

"Does she believe you?" said Scotty.

"Cass?" said Edee.

"Yeah."

"No."

"Exactly." Scotty dropped his head against the back of the sofa, feigning boredom.

Edee busied herself with another chip and hoped he would drop it.

A few moments later, Scotty said, "Jonathan Watch was negative again this afternoon. I think we should go round other optician's, see if anyone else knows him." He leaned forward and took another bite of burger.

LATER THAT EVENING, Edee couldn't stop thinking about the fact that she and Lucie hadn't spoken about the lines since that Saturday in the cafe. A few months back it would have been unthinkable for something so big to be going on and for Lucie to not know everything about it. Should she have tried again, found another way to explain it to her? Maybe. Or should she have waited longer before telling her? The lines, the lights, were all so ordinary now, so every day, that she'd have been able to tell her much more calmly. Perhaps that would have made a difference. Then again, how she told her shouldn't have been the point.

Lucie should have been interested no matter how clear Edee had been.

What if things never got back to how they were? What if she did nothing and regretted it forever? Grabbing her phone, she began typing. The message was short but clear and to the point. *You know the lines (glasses thing), more's happened. Do you want to hear about it? I want to tell you.* She tapped send.

A few minutes later, she put the phone on her bedside shelf but her eyes were not able to leave it alone. Perhaps the three of them were out somewhere with no reception again. Or perhaps Rosa and Greg were insisting on another phone-free evening. Or perhaps she really wasn't interested. Perhaps Edee had not known her as well as she thought she had. Thudding her feet to the floor, she headed to the kitchen for a glass of water.

Mum was in her office sorting through some samples. Squares of tiles and fabric covered the floor. As Edee passed for the second time, Mum said, "Dinner was good, wasn't it?"

Edee stopped. "Yeah."

"I thought I'd invite them over here again at the weekend. You're okay with that, aren't you?"

"Sure."

"He's juggling so much, poor man," said Mum. "So many firsts he'd never imagined. I feel for him. I really do." Her phone rang. She glanced over but did not reach for it. "Life can be so difficult. He apologised to me that the food wasn't homemade." She shook her head. "It was just lovely to see them."

Yes, thought Edee, and also . . . Mum never ignored her phone. The lines over her body were glittering strongly. Wait. Mum was worried about Craig. *Craig and Mum?* Was that what Mum was thinking? Really? No, she wouldn't. She couldn't. Jo had only been gone a few weeks. And Mum had worked with him for years. He was an accountant. He was . . . Edee shook her head. *No.* Mum wanted to help him, that was all. She was being nice.

"I think we'll make it the weekend, then they can stay a bit later again," said Mum, pulling a square of fabric from one row to another and then laying it on a tile. "He's got to work next week. Perhaps Saturday. Have you got any plans?"

"No," said Edee.

"Good." She pulled a second piece of fabric towards the first and sat back on her heels. Her toes clicked. "There was something else. I wanted to say I'm proud of you."

Edee took a mouthful of water. The tile was terracotta. The two fabric squares were pink. She would never have put them together.

Mum picked up another tile. "The way you've been with Scotty. It means a lot to me, and Craig appreciates it as well. He told me tonight. He thinks it's helping."

Edee swallowed. She wasn't even thirsty. Not really.

"I know it's helping you too," said Mum. "Lucie is lovely, but she isn't here."

Edee's mind went straight back to her empty phone screen. Her fingers squeezed the glass.

"Scotty is," said Mum. "And that's good. I'm proud. I wanted you to know."

"Okay," said Edee.

"I could drop you two at the cinema if you like, after we've eaten," said Mum. "Or before. Have a think about it."

"Okay," said Edee again. She began to move. Mum thought she'd been right about the friends thing, but she was wrong too. It wasn't *friends*; it was Scotty. He was different. She liked him a lot, but he wasn't Lucie. It wasn't that simple. None of this was simple. When she got back to her room, the phone screen remained unchanged.

It was the same in the morning. Edee sat in the kitchen forcing herself to eat a slice of toast while Mum ignored another call. Two in two days. A new sense of unease dropped into the depths of her stomach. Mum had no business being different. Not Mum *and* Lucie. It wasn't fair. It . . . wasn't only unease. It was foreboding, anticipation. Something was going on and that meant—her mind leapt and leapt again—something to do with the lines. They'd been the start of all the extra weirdness. It felt like some kind of new premonition, a precursor to everything notching up another level.

All that day and the next, Edee kept expecting them to suddenly reveal something more, an epic beyond the epic. But they didn't. They carried on as they always did, shining and glittering and glowing.

Nothing happened.

Nothing.

She began to think she'd been mistaken. The foreboding started to ebb away. By Saturday evening it had all but gone.

And then she opened the door expecting to see Craig, Scotty, and Amber and found, instead, that the space before her was filled—*impossibly*—by Lucie and Rosa.

28

It was as if she had opened the door on a mirage. The one thing she had wanted for so long was here. *There.* An arm's length away. And yet, how could it be? And why? Her airway clogged up with dread, expectation, hope. She looked from one to the other and back again. Lucie and Rosa were both, of course, covered in shining and glittering lines. It was the least unexpected thing going on right then.

"Hi," said Lucie.

"What . . ." began Edee. Was this even real? *Was* it a mirage?

"Edee," said Rosa. "It's so good to see you. May we come in?"

May we come in? Even in the middle of her confusion, Edee could feel her face etching with a deeper layer of incomprehension. Rosa, old-Rosa, would never have said 'may we come in'. She'd have been dishing out hugs and walking inside without waiting for any invitation.

Edee took a step back. Her fingers were still curled around the handle. She glanced behind, anticipating Mum's appearance a split second before she was there. The surprise she saw across her face was at least confirmation this was actually happening.

"Rosa?" said Mum. "Lucie?"

"Gen." Rosa stepped forward into the hallway. Lucie did too, a little behind.

Edee closed the door. She turned around slowly and looked to her friend. Lucie must have been aware of that, she was so, so close, but she made no sign, no hint of acknowledgement and no attempt to help Edee out. Instead, she was looking at Mum like she'd never seen her before.

"This is unexpected," said Mum. "Edee, did you . . . ?"

Perhaps she saw the surprise replicated in her daughter's face and did not, therefore, feel the need to finish the question. Edee murmured, "No," anyway.

Mum nodded. She and Rosa seemed to lock eyes for a moment or two. Lucie looked towards the ceiling.

"Is Greg . . . ?" said Mum.

"In Slovenia," said Rosa. "He's fine, thank you."

Once again, Edee glanced towards Lucie—she hadn't really stopped looking at her—but Lucie was still not meeting her gaze. It was so un-Lucie like that Edee's mind filled with imposters, and aliens, and all sorts of other crazy explanations.

There was silence for a few moments. Awkward silence. Then Mum said, "Come through." She seemed unsure whether to turn into the kitchen or the lounge. She chose the lounge. "Would you like a drink, or . . . ?"

"Yes," said Rosa. "Thank you."

"Tea?" said Mum. "I think we still have some green from . . ."

Before, finished Edee silently. From the time when Rosa had come round so often that Mum had kept a box of her favourite drink in the cupboard.

"Lovely," said Rosa.

"Lucie," said Mum. "Breakfast?"

"Great," said Lucie. In the whole of their thirteen years of friendship, she had never said so few words. It barely sounded like her.

Mum headed towards the kitchen and Edee found herself saying, "What's going on?"

Rosa linked her fingers together and settled them on her lap. The knuckles paled. Her lines glittered. "It's so good to see you. Let's wait for your mum to come back, shall we?"

No, thought Edee, let's not. She began to turn. "I'll go and help." Her phone, on the sideboard, flashed with a message. She walked straight past.

As soon as she reached the kitchen, Mum—her lines shining so much that Edee squinted—said, "What's this about? Have you any idea?"

"No," said Edee. And although that was true, all of a sudden she felt as if she were on an invisible tightrope. Whatever happened, Mum was going to realise that things between her and Lucie had changed (she probably already had; Lucie hadn't *looked* at her) and she was going to want to know why.

"Lucie hasn't said?" The kettle grew louder and Mum moved towards the hob, lifting the lid on one saucepan and stirring a second.

"No." Edee turned towards the cupboard and took out four mugs. Her hands were shaking.

"THANK YOU," said Rosa, a few minutes later as Mum balanced the tray on the coffee table and moved the mugs across onto the wooden coaster mats.

There was another silence.

Edee took one of the teas and wrapped her hands

around the bowl. It was hot, too hot, but she kept them there anyway.

"How long are you back for?" said Mum. She was in the bucket chair. The visitors were on the sofa.

"A couple of nights," said Rosa. "We fly again on Monday morning."

"I see," said Mum.

Fly? Edee felt a new wave of confusion. The version of Rosa and Greg that had left in a camper van were anti-flying. It was one of the reasons they'd bought the van in the first place.

Mum was leaning on the arm of the chair. "Has something happened to your parents? Your brother?"

"No," said Rosa. "They don't know we're back, actually."

"Right," said Mum. "I . . . if we'd known we could have prepared something. But we . . . this is so unexpected . . . What's going on?"

Rosa nodded, as if she was finally admitting this whole situation was indeed peculiar. She re-clasped her fingers. "You see, we've been concerned. Increasingly concerned and we—I—thought a face-to-face visit would be—"

"Concerned?" said Mum. "About what?"

There was another silence. Edee could hear the blood pulsing against her eardrums.

"About Edee," said Rosa.

The blood was pulsing in her stomach too.

Lucie was still looking anywhere but at her.

"Edee?" said Mum.

Rosa nodded slowly. "You know we've always considered her family."

Mum was staring.

"And a while back Lucie mentioned something to us that

seemed out of character. We thought it might be a phase, with the changes, and we—"

Mum's lips had flattened.

"—anyway, recently Lucie came to us again, rightly, and we—Greg and I—felt we could not sit back any longer."

There was another silence. Mum's foot was bobbing up and down now. The room was lit up with lines. There were so, so many. Edee's own hands around the mug were radiating light as if she'd turned into a sun, one of four independent, elongated suns. The space barely seemed capable of containing them.

"What, exactly, are you concerned about?" said Mum. "Given the circumstances"—the word could not have been more loaded—"I think she's responded admirably. More, in fact. Given you have not been here, you would not know that of course."

Rosa leaned forward and picked up her mug. She rested the edge of it on her knee. "There's no judgment, Gen. None at all. We love Edee like she's part of our family, you know that. She *is*, that's why we're here. I think, well, perhaps it can sometimes take somebody from outside to pick up on these things. I know you would do the same for us, for Lucie."

Mum's foot had stilled.

Edee felt sick.

"Let me explain," said Rosa, "A while back, Edee confided in Lucie that she has been experiencing something unusual. A visual disturbance."

There was a new, heavier silence. Then Mum said, "A visual disturbance?"

Rosa nodded. "We thought it might be a phase, something like a stress response. And it did seem to settle down. However, a few days ago Lucie received a message from

Edee that suggested otherwise and we felt we must intervene."

"What, exactly, do you mean by a visual disturbance?" said Mum.

"She has been seeing things," said Rosa. She turned so that her body and face were pointed towards Edee. "We're all here for you. I understand this is difficult. Are you able to say more or would you like me to?"

Whether she wanted to was not the point. Edee was unable, right then, to speak at all. She'd thought her feelings towards Rosa could not have got any worse. She could not have been more wrong. Rosa had taken something—something that was not her business—shaken it up, twisted it, and delivered it here three times the size and in a completely different shape. To *Mum*. Rosa had no idea.

"Seeing things?" said Mum. "Seeing what? Edee? What's she talking about?"

"We're all here for you," said Rosa again. Her tone had lowered, as if she were speaking to an injured, unpredictable animal.

And Edee's voice reappeared. "She doesn't understand."

"That's a yes?" said Rosa.

Lucie was now wearing an expression that Edee had never, ever seen before on anyone. It was as if her face was frozen between a hundred emotions.

"Edee?" said Mum.

"Yes," said Edee. "But it's not bad." As the words left her mouth, she wished she could push them back in. Mum had sent her to a counsellor for way, way less. This was *Mum*. There was no chance she was going to believe that. She should have said no. Mum would've wanted to believe no.

But she couldn't lie about this. She couldn't. She wouldn't.

There was another pause. Mum and Rosa were both looking at Edee and Lucie was still looking anywhere *but* at her. Not lying was one thing but this was impossible. Whatever she said now was going to sound wrong. The room itself felt like it was full of electricity and that whatever words she came up with would be the spark that ignited the place, the spark that sent the suns to some irrevocable place. She chewed her lip and wished for a miracle.

For the second time that evening, the doorbell rang.

Seconds ticked by. No one said anything. Then Edee slowly, as if she was expecting someone to pin her down at any moment, got up. She left the room as Mum said something that began with, "Tonight, we—"

Edee carried on walking and opened the front door. This time, the space outside was filled, as it was supposed to be, by Scotty, Craig, and Amber.

"Hello," said Craig. He had the baby in one arm and a bottle in the other. Amber was clutching a bag of chocolates and squeezing the wrapper over and over. "We've been so looking forward to this."

"Hey," said Scotty.

"We've been trying to explain curry to Amber," said Craig. "It's impossible, we discovered. She's going to have to taste it."

Edee stepped back. The three of them moved inside.

"Is everything alright?" said Craig, as he slipped his shoes off.

"Yeah," said Edee. She was still holding the mug.

Scotty, a pace behind his dad, mouthed, "What's up?" He splayed a hand's worth of fingers towards himself. "Lines?"

Edee nodded, raised her eyebrows, and glanced towards the other two spare pairs of shoes.

Mum appeared at the other end of the hallway.

"Gen," said Craig. "We're so looking forward to this, aren't we Amber?"

The baby gurgled.

Mum looked worried.

Edee headed towards the lounge as if everything was completely normal. She could feel Scotty following her. Rosa was now in the lounge doorway. Edee carried on walking and Rosa stepped into the hall.

Lucie—*finally*—looked up. Her eyes were full of surprise. "Who are you?"

"Scotty Leigh. Who are you?"

"Lucie." Her face dropped again, like she remembered the last five minutes.

"Lucie?" said Scotty. "Camper van Lucie?"

"Yes," said Edee. Lucie was now looking at her, confused, and she found herself adding, "Stuff has changed here too. You'd know that if you'd been speaking to me and not telling tales to your mum."

Creases appeared at the edge of Lucie's eyes. "It wasn't tales. I had to."

"No, you didn't," said Edee.

Scotty made a noise like a backwards whistle. "Things just got interesting, am I right?"

29

"Things got unnecessary," said Edee.

"Unnecessary? You're *seeing* things," said Lucie.

"The camper van disbeliever is what I'm seeing," said Scotty.

Lucie stared at him. Edee had seen her do that a million times before. More often than not she'd found it funny. She'd *admired* it. Fierce Lucie. The person who had always been on her side. This time it was different. It was . . . not admirable.

"I had to say something," said Lucie.

"No you didn't," said Edee.

"Yes I did," said Lucie. "I'm your best friend."

"You promised you wouldn't," said Edee, "but you told your mum and dad anyway. And Cass and Maddie."

"I didn't promise," said Lucie.

Edee stared this time. Yes, she had. Hadn't she? Edee had told her to promise and Lucie had said . . . well, she couldn't remember but, by virtue of being Lucie, she had promised.

"And you didn't tell me it was going to be something so big," said Lucie. "What was I supposed to do?"

"Believe me," said Edee.

"You're seeing things," said Lucie. "No one would believe that."

"Not true," said Scotty.

Lucie shot him a second look.

"Just saying." Scotty lifted his hands a touch.

"You could've talked to me," said Edee.

"I did," said Lucie.

"No you didn't," said Edee. "For ages you didn't at all and then only when Cass and Maddie were around."

"So that they knew what was going on," said Lucie. "We were looking out for you."

Edee shook her head.

Seconds ticked on by.

Uncertain voices were coming from the hallway. One hunched. One low. One grating. Edee had never noticed the harsh, uncompromising edge to Rosa's voice before.

"Look," said Craig, a little louder, "we'll go, give you some space, but if you need anything, and I mean anything, then—"

"No," said Mum. "You're here for dinner. It was arranged. It's ready. You're staying."

"It smells wonderful," said Craig.

"We have plans," continued Mum. "If you'd told us you were coming. If you—"

"I tried," said Rosa. "You know I did. I called. I left messages. I said it was important."

Oh. Edee pulled her sleeves over her hands and curled her fingers in the cuffs.

"Gen, we're worried. I can understand it's hard for you to take this in, but Edee is experiencing some kind of psychological disturbance and ignoring it is—"

"Yet my daughter's psychological wellbeing was not on your radar when you decided to separate her from her best friend," said Mum. "What makes you think that—"

"I can't leave this," said Rosa. "I won't."

"I don't think it is up to you," said Mum. "You walked away."

"Drove," said Scotty.

"Gen," said Rosa.

"No," said Mum.

"Ignoring this is . . ." began Rosa. "We came back. For you. For Edee."

"For two nights," said Mum. "And, for your information, I am not ignoring my daughter's psychological wellbeing."

"Then did you know she's been seeing things?" said Rosa. "Because to my knowledge she has only confided in Lucie. We're here for you. For both of you."

Edee could almost hear Mum shaking her head.

Amber gurgled.

"Should we," said Craig, his voice lower again but still audible, "should we hear what Edee has to say about this, because—"

"She admitted it just before you arrived," said Rosa.

Edee closed her eyes for a second. *Admitted*. It sounded so wrong.

Craig cleared his throat. "It's just, she seems so . . ."

"Well," said Mum. "Exactly. Fine, let's talk and then we'll get on with our evening."

Scotty sat down and leaned against the wall. He smiled.

Edee had never felt less like smiling.

The lounge suddenly became a lot more full. Rosa returned to the sofa, Craig and Amber took the bucket seat, and Mum perched on the footrest. Edee was left standing. She knelt down. The four suns had become six. She looked to the floor.

"We're all here for you," said Rosa. "All of us. You were telling us about the things you've been seeing. Could you start there again?" She was back to speaking in the injured animal tone.

Edee looked up and met her eyes. "I was saying it's not bad."

"But you have been seeing things?" said Rosa.

"I'm able to see something I couldn't before," said Edee.

"How long has this been going on?" said Mum.

"Since I got my glasses," said Edee.

Mum's face visibly relaxed. "You're seeing with more clarity, more sharpness. This fuss is about you getting glasses?"

Edee nodded.

"No it isn't," said Lucie. "You're seeing lines. Glasses don't make you see that."

Scotty sucked in a breath. "Ouch."

"Lines?" said Mum. "What do you mean, lines?"

It was like the lounge, the bright, bright lounge, had become a trap, a cell. It was impossible to say nothing, yet if she got up and left it would look to them like she was guilty of something, and if she told them the truth, well, some kind of chaos would follow. She was fairly sure the doorbell was not going to save her this time, and it was clear that Lucie was not going to either. Edee's throat ached. She swallowed. "Lines of light."

"Light?" said Mum.

"Around people." Telling them felt miserable. It was so, so far from the way it had felt to tell Scotty. Rosa was leaning in like this was some kind of confession, and the vertical worry lines were back on Mum's forehead, creating a peculiar checkerboard effect with the horizontal glittering.

"They circle people," said Edee.

"Why didn't you say they were faulty?" said Mum. "At that price."

"They glitter and change," said Edee. "They're interesting."

Rosa leaned even further forward. "What do you mean when you say glitter and change?"

Edee almost said, *glitter and change*. Instead, she swallowed those words away, looked Rosa in the eyes, and said, "Like they're alive."

"Alive?" said Mum.

"She can see them without the glasses too," said Lucie. "She said they're on everyone."

Amid the disbelief that Lucie would say that right now, Edee couldn't help but think *not babies*. The inaccuracy was as confusing as everything else. Lucie hadn't listened or she hadn't cared?

"Did the optician raise any concerns about your eyes?" said Craig.

Mum shook her head.

"Someone I worked with once had a problem with their retina," said Craig. "He saw all sorts of colours. Incredible was how he described it. Extreme colours. Could it be something like that? Perhaps it's some sort of minor version, a symptom?"

Edee shook her head.

"He's fine now," said Craig. "After treatment. It might be worth a return visit to the optician's, or the hospital, just to be sure."

"I said that," said Lucie. "She wouldn't."

"We went back," said Scotty. "I went with her."

Lucie shot another look his way.

Edee turned to look at him too, willing him not to mention the invisible optician. Not right now.

"What happened?" said Mum.

"We spoke to the woman on the counter," said Scotty. "It was really interesting."

"But you didn't see an optician?" said Mum.

"No." Edee's insides were squirming . . . but Mum had been there too. She'd seen the man. She knew he was real.

"They said there was no one called Jonathan who worked there," said Scotty. "That's why it was interesting."

"How did you know his name?" said Mum.

"He told us," said Edee. Mum had *been there*.

"The woman swore he didn't work there," said Scotty.

"He fitted the glasses," said Mum. "That's all."

"She said he couldn't have," said Scotty.

"He's probably called something different at work," said Craig. "Let's not go to the conspiracy theories."

Scotty raised his eyebrows. "I'm only saying what she said. Things aren't adding up."

"It's not the glasses anyway," said Lucie. "She's seeing them all the time."

Edee's eyes swung to the left. This new travelling version of Lucie seemed to have developed a loose jaw.

"Is that true?" said Mum.

Edee nodded.

"Are you getting headaches?" said Mum.

"Migraine auras." Craig nodded. "That crossed my mind too. Do you remember Erica Johns? She used to get them most months." Amber had been squirming in his lap. He leaned forward and put her on the floor. She rolled to all fours and babbled.

"Why does it have to be something you already know about?" said Scotty. "Why can't it be something new?"

"Scotty," said Craig. "Not now."

Rosa was leaning so far forward that she seemed in danger of falling off the sofa. "Edee, when you said circling people, what did you mean exactly?"

"The lines cover their body," said Edee. Your body, she added in her head.

Rosa made an odd noise. "I didn't realise. I'm starting to wonder, well, if all the changes could have released a latent ability in you and you're seeing auras. Energy, you know. Recently I—"

"Wait," said Mum, raising a hand. "Let me get this straight. Ten minutes ago, you walked into our home insisting that my daughter had a major problem and suggesting that I—the person who has been by her side over the last six turbulent months—have been neglecting her health. Now you're suggesting she's some sort of psychic? I'm . . . Rosa. How can you think this is acceptable? How can you—"

"I'm trying to help," said Rosa. "We both are and—"

"Help what?" said Mum. "Who? You? That's all I'm seeing. Turning up here trying to play some hero in a situation that's the direct consequences of your selfish actions."

Rosa shook her head. "Not this again. We chose to show Lucie how much more there is in the world. Expanding her horizons and ours too and—"

"In one direction," said Scotty. "On one plane."

"It's brilliant," said Lucie. "You have no idea."

"You could have come with us," said Rosa. "You know we invited you."

"I'm not going to take my child out of school the year before her exams," said Mum.

"Travelling is more than an education," said Rosa.

"Never mind the disruption left behind," said Mum. "Leave that to other people to sort out."

Rosa said something else, then Mum, then Craig. It was babble, noise.

The light in the room was glittering so strongly. Music,

thought Edee again. Six people playing six different, silent songs at once. A silent orchestra.

The lights began to blur, each line becoming a little less distinct, and somehow Edee found herself to be above everything, as if she were lying on her back on the ceiling looking down on the room. But she couldn't be because she was down there too, sitting on the floor within her own ball of light. It was impossible, yet impossible didn't seem important and the question floated away. There were seven people down there and six balls of light. Six balls of light made up of thousands and thousands of lines. Lines that had grown out of the six heads and spun themselves around the attached bodies; a tight covering, a film. A film made from lines, which were made from words that had melted together. The words were not readable, of course, yet everything was there in the picture. A picture of a million words or more.

The room itself began to shrink in size then, and the street was there with more and more people inside their people-sized suns. Then that street melted into two streets, three, four, more, and into the town. Then the town melted into the next, and those into cities, the county, the country, the world. Tiny, smaller-than-ant-sized lights were scurrying about. It was so, so clear. So unbelievably clear.

So unbelievably calm.

There was nothing but the calm.

Then there was nothing but the room and the six people and the one baby, who was sitting in the midst of them all, gazing up at something over Edee's shoulder.

And no lines, *none*.

Edee started, blinked, and each set flickered back. The people were talking still. The babble was louder. The lines were glittering so much it was as if there were small fires everywhere yet nothing, nothing, nothing was burning.

She blinked again. Mum and Rosa were in the middle of a heated exchange, with Craig trying to chip in. He was standing up now. Lucie and Scotty were glaring at each other from opposite sides of the room.

Edee stood, slowly turned around, walked into the hall, slipped her feet into some shoes and, for the third time that evening, opened the front door.

30

S he did not go down. Instead, she headed towards the narrow staircase at the opposite end of the corridor. The door to the roof terrace was usually locked, yet as Edee reached the top step and slipped the two bolts back she knew it wasn't going to be. It wasn't.

The space out here was small, much smaller than the footprint of the building. It was also unfamiliar. For years Mum had not allowed her anywhere near it, and even though that had changed since the place had been renovated, Edee had never been particularly interested in it anyway. Right now, however, there was something about the height that was drawing her in, as if this place might possibly get her a tiny bit closer to wherever it was she had been a few minutes ago. The perspective here was much, much less than that had been, but she could see the streets rolling out and the toy-sized, sun-covered people moving in all directions.

She could feel—sense—the sheer similarity of everything, of *everybody*, looking out at the world through the filter of their person-sized wrappers. The lines were different, but they all *had* lines.

It was epic and normal, enormous and minuscule, her and not her all at once. She, whoever that was, had no idea what all this was about and an intense understanding of it at the same time. Fish in water. Humans in great, glittering balls of light.

They were okay; she was, the others were. Lucie was. And Amber, the baby who, most likely, would one day be covered just like them.

But before everything else, before the noise, the music, the light, the chatter, they were okay. All of them.

And some even knew that. Like Kitty, who knew but didn't know; who maybe hadn't seen the lines but had a sense of the thing, Edee was sure.

The sun—the yellow, light-giving, heat-bringing one above—was beginning to set. The sky ran from a muted, greyish-blue to a spread of orange and the moon was visible too. The space above seemed so huge, so unknowable, and yet so there. She sat in the middle of the decking and lay back, resting her head on her palms, looking up into the sky; into whatever it was the sky was made out of.

"SHE'S HERE." The shout seemed muffled at first. Other sounds followed, louder, more distinct. There were feet perhaps, and other words, different voices. Then Mum called, "Don't do anything stupid, Edee. Don't move. Don't move an inch."

Move? Edee opened her eyes. The surface under her was hard and the space above was a deep, deep blue with little lights here and there. She was . . . outside, that was right.

Lying down. What did moving have to do with anything? The next moment Mum was above her, towering, coming closer, kneeling. Her eyes, even in the low light out here, had a hollow, haunted look to them. She was clutching Edee's phone in her hand. Then Craig was there and Rosa, and over to the side were Scotty and Lucie. Amber was in Scotty's arms.

Edee yawned.

Mum leaned forward. Her hands were on Edee's shoulders, the phone pressing against her right side, and she was staring into her eyes as if she could see through them to the inner workings of her brain. "Whatever possessed you to come up here? What were you doing? Where did you get a key?"

"She's alright, Gen," said Craig. His hand was on Mum's shoulder. "We've found her. She's safe."

Safe, wondered Edee. Of course she was safe.

"It's so dangerous up here," said Mum. "I've had nightmares about this place and you . . . You didn't even bring your phone."

Dangerous? The terrace was back from the roof edge and each side was framed by a see-through barrier. Edee was lying down in the middle of the decking.

"Why are you lying down?" said Mum. "Are you ill? Do you have a headache? Were you—

"I was looking at the sunset," said Edee. "And then . . . I fell asleep."

"You fell asleep," said Mum. "Up here? Thank God you're not a sleepwalker. What if you'd started tonight? I can't bear to think about it." She let go of Edee's shoulders and sank to the decking, running a hand over her forehead. "We're supposed to be eating curry."

Craig knelt down. "It's alright, she's here. She's fine." He looked over. "Are you? Do you feel sick? Dizzy?"

"I'm . . . great," said Edee.

Mum made a low, groaning sound. "Why did you leave?"

Edee chewed her lip. How could she explain? She couldn't. She'd got a pair of glasses and the whole world had changed, elevated. It didn't even have anything to do with the glasses. But for the look on Mum's face, she would have laughed.

Mum rubbed the sides of her head. "I have no idea what's going on. This evening is—"

"You were fighting . . ." began Edee. She sat up. No. There was no point going there. "I'm fine, really. I didn't mean to worry you. I just . . . I wanted some air. I didn't mean to fall asleep."

Mum lifted her head. She shook it. "But the roof? I have no idea what to think."

"Let's go downstairs," said Craig. He took Edee's phone and held it out, then helped Mum up, nudging her towards the doorway, before glancing back at Edee. She was already on her feet. He raised an eyebrow as if asking a question. Edee nodded. The lines covering him, she noticed, were slightly less intense than usual.

"Make sure it's closed," said Craig. It might have been directed at any one of them.

Rosa stepped back as Mum and Craig passed. Lucie turned and followed them.

"That was some exit," said Scotty, as Edee drew level with him. "Jonathan-like."

"I didn't mean to," said Edee. "It was . . ."

"I said you'd be alright." Scotty nudged her shoulder. "They thought I knew where you were."

The two of them moved back inside. Behind them, Rosa pulled the door shut and slipped the bolts across with a metallic grating.

"Something else happened, right?" muttered Scotty.

"Yeah," said Edee.

"Tell," said Scotty. He leaned closer. "And also, we are so going out there in the summer. How come you never said your building has a room on the roof?"

"Mum will probably get it permanently boarded up now," said Edee.

Scotty laughed. "We'd been all over looking for you. Then there you were, lying like a comatose thing on the decking."

"I was asleep," said Edee.

"Epic," said Scotty. "Here." He handed the now-sleeping Amber across. "I've been carrying her for an hour. I swear she's heavier when she sleeps."

The baby was warm and solid and very, very there.

"So, what happened?" said Scotty.

Edee hugged Amber a little tighter. She stepped to the side, waiting for Rosa to pass by. The woman hesitated then increased her pace, her eyes on Lucie's back. "I don't know. I saw all of you, all of us, inside the balls of light. Only I was outside myself too. It was . . . the lines are there and not there. They're us but not us."

Scotty's eyes were wide. "Oh man." The next second his face dropped. "Why can't that stuff happen to me?" His lines glittered.

The two of them began moving again. With every step Edee wanted to say *it is*, but she didn't and then the front door was ahead, open. They passed through it. Mum was there. The look she gave felt like another x-ray.

Rosa was picking up her bag. Lucie was standing with her arms crossed.

"We'll go," said Rosa. "Now she's back, and . . ."

Mum's lips were pressed flat again.

"Stay," said Edee. "Have some curry." It felt like five

pairs of eyes swivelled to rest on her. "There's loads. It's okay, isn't it?"

"I . . . it's probably spoiled," said Mum. "Overcooked. The rice will be terrible."

There was a pause, a heavy, heavy silence.

"We'll cook some more," said Edee.

"Are you sure that's what you want?" said Rosa.

"Sure," said Edee.

"Gen?" said Rosa.

Mum said nothing. Her brows were pulled together.

"It's only dinner," said Edee.

Craig lifted the little girl from her arms. "Let me put Amber in her cot and I'll come and help."

Mum, massaging the sides of her head again, moved towards the kitchen.

"I should call Greg," said Rosa. "Let him know." She slipped her phone from her bag and headed towards the lounge.

Lucie had not moved. She seemed shiny and small. Edee took a step closer. "Luce?"

Lucie's face screwed up. "What's going on? Are we pretending you're not seeing stuff now?"

"No," said Edee. "We can talk about the lines if you want. Or not. It doesn't matter."

"We can talk about them tomorrow," said Scotty. "Or the day after."

Lucie shot him another look. "Who *are* you?"

Edee had never heard her sound so unfriendly, so uninterested in somebody. She wanted to hug her but Lucie stepped back.

"Scotty," said Scotty. "We met a couple of hours ago."

"The boy you were eating chips with?" said Lucie.

"Yeah," said Edee.

"Cass told me," said Lucie. "You didn't."

"We've been hanging out," said Edee. "That's all."

"Does he know you've seen stuff growing from people's heads?" said Lucie.

Edee nodded.

"And I think it's awesome," said Scotty.

Lucie looked from one to the other. She turned and headed into the bathroom, closing the door with a decisive click.

THEY ATE IN THE KITCHEN. It was a squeeze for six, but the table had already been laid. Mum added another couple of settings to the edge of the counter and she and Craig sat there, a little higher, a little detached. The room felt full of something other than bodies. It was odd. Didn't they get that everything was as it should be? If only they'd seen what she'd seen.

The conversation started and stopped over and over. The cutlery clunked on the china.

"What's been the best part of travelling so far?" Edee asked, when the latest pause had stretched and stretched.

Rosa glanced to Mum, who was focusing on her plate. "We don't need to talk about it now."

"Why?" said Edee. "You're really into it."

Rosa put a spoonful of curry in her mouth and chewed it slowly. "All of it, Edee. It's hard to pick one."

"Do you have a favourite country?" said Edee.

"Not really," said Rosa. "I like them all for different reasons."

"What about you?" said Edee. There was another long, heavy pause as if her friend had not heard.

"Lucie?" said Rosa.

"All of it," said Lucie. She snapped a poppadum and

dipped it in the sauce. "We're all liking it so much we might not come back."

"No," said Rosa.

"What?" said Lucie. "You and Dad have said that. Europe this year, Asia next."

Rosa put down her fork and picked up her glass. "Nothing's finalised. We've been throwing around some ideas, that's all."

There was another silence.

"Our money's lasting longer than we thought," said Rosa, as if someone had asked for an explanation. "And we've both picked up some work along the way. You can live on very little, we've learned."

Craig cleared his throat.

"But as I said, nothing's finalised. We do realise we have responsibilities."

Mum shook her head.

"What?" said Rosa.

"You used to," said Mum. "Yet we—Edee—has been recovering from the last upset, then you turn up and she ends up on the roof."

"It didn't have anything to do with them," said Edee.

"I beg to differ," said Mum.

"Everything's fine," said Edee.

"You were on the roof," said Mum.

"I was looking at the sky," said Edee.

"Now you're saying that you might not be coming back," said Mum. "And I'll be picking up those pieces too."

"There aren't any pieces," said Edee. "I'm good, really."

"We might not come back and you don't care," said Lucie. "You're different."

"I do care," said Edee. "I still miss you."

"You've got a boyfriend and you didn't tell me," said Lucie.

213

"He's not my boyfriend," said Edee.

"I don't believe you," said Lucie. "And you never told me about him." She looked to her mum. "Everything's different here."

"Things move on," said Rosa. "It wouldn't be reasonable to expect everything to stand still." She twisted in her seat. "Edee, you're welcome to come and visit us any time. I hope we made that clear. Whatever's going on with you, or us, our door's always open."

"Just a plane ride away," muttered Mum.

Rosa picked up her fork again. "Craig, I'm sorry, I don't feel we've had much chance to be introduced. How do you know Gen and Edee?"

"Oh," said Craig. "From years ago. We used to work together at Veronica's. We'd lost touch. And we bumped into each other a few weeks ago."

"That's nice," said Rosa.

"Yes." Craig shook his head a little. "The timing was perfect. She's been such a support. Edee too. We've, well, it's been a difficult time."

Rosa nodded. "Life's full of ups and downs as they say."

Mum shook her head again.

"Who're they?" said Scotty. "Who says?"

"Scotty," said Craig.

"What?" Scotty sat taller. "It's a good question."

"My wife left," said Craig. "It's been challenging. Scotty likes to question things."

"Not because of Mum," said Scotty.

"No," said Craig. "I know."

"I can't believe you've dropped me so quickly," said Lucie.

"I haven't," said Edee.

Something flashed across Lucie's face. "You're seeing

things. How come everyone's forgetting that? I don't understand what's going on."

Lines in all directions were glittering.

"I can promise you I have not forgotten anything that's gone on this evening," said Mum.

"Why aren't you angry?" Lucie's eyebrows were knitted together. She was facing Edee but talking to the table. "You were angry before. Why aren't you now?"

"I'm just not," said Edee.

"And you think that's bad?" said Scotty.

"It doesn't make sense," said Lucie.

The phone in Edee's pocket vibrated. She took it out and read the message, as much for the pause it offered as anything else. Lucie's also chimed an alert.

It was Cass: *Lucie! Oh my God!!! You have to meet Ty. He's working tomorrow. Meet at 11. We can use his discount. I can't believe you're back. Whaaaat! xxx*

The cafe. Kitty. Edee looked to Lucie, who was concentrating on her phone. Her eyebrows were still drawn together.

"Something important?" said Rosa.

Lucie didn't say anything.

"Cass wants Lucie to meet Ty tomorrow," said Edee. "Her boyfriend."

Rosa nodded. "We should make the most of being here."

"I don't want to," said Lucie.

"Nonsense," said Rosa. "We have one more day here, you should see Cass and Maddie. Catch up face to face while we have the opportunity."

"I didn't mean that," said Lucie.

"I want to," said Edee.

"Scotty, you should join them," said Mum. She glanced

to Craig. "I'm sorry about this evening. Why don't you drop Scotty round here and come up for coffee."

"I'd be glad to," said Craig. "Thank you." He reached across for Mum's empty plate and stacked it on his.

Scotty leaned back and drummed his fingers on the table.

Lucie shot him another look.

31

"I don't get how come you two are friends," said Scotty.

It was the next morning. They'd just left the apartment building.

"I can't remember not being friends with her," said Edee. "She's not usually like she was yesterday."

"Grumpy and mean?" said Scotty. "Girls like her give girls a bad name."

"She's alright," said Edee. She was watching her and Scotty's lines flickering as they walked. It was so weird. Her two realities had collided, were colliding. Never in a million years could she have imagined walking with him to meet the others; never in a zillion years would she have thought she'd be totally fine about it.

"Did you get a lecture last night?" said Scotty. "About the roof."

"No," said Edee. "Mum didn't really say much after you left."

"Dad did," said Scotty. "He said Rosa reminded him of Mum. He said it all the way home, like he thought if he said it enough I'd agree with him." Scotty shook his head. "She's nothing like her. I'm nothing like Lucie."

Except for having lines. That made them similar. "Do you mind meeting the others?"

"No," said Scotty. "But I'm here because I want to be around when you have another pre-roof thing. If you disappear off, I'm going to be right there. I want to see stuff too."

Edee didn't correct him. Scotty being there was fine by her. She was going to introduce him to Kitty to see if he got there was something different about her. She couldn't believe she hadn't thought to introduce them before.

———

"You're Scotty?" said Cass, a few minutes later. She had looked him up and down in a Cass kind of way, appraising.

"Yep," said Scotty. "You're Cass?"

"Yeah."

"Impressive powers of deduction, right?" said Scotty.

"No," said Cass. "Edes probably showed you a picture."

"She didn't," said Scotty.

Cass glanced over her shoulder towards Ty, who was serving someone at the counter. "I can't wait to see Lucie. She's coming with Maddie. How come she didn't come with you?"

Edee shrugged. There didn't seem much point getting into yesterday. Lucie was okay, she knew that. This would blow over. She scanned the room. Kitty didn't seem to be out here yet. "Is Ty working all day?"

"Until five," said Cass, glancing back again. "We're thinking of a film later if Lucie's up for it. At mine, maybe."

"Great," said Edee. She scanned the room more slowly.

"Oh my God!" Cass rushed past both of them and wrapped herself around Lucie. "I cannot believe you're here. I'm not even mad you didn't tell us. It's the best surprise. Come and meet Ty properly. You're going to love him."

"Hi," said Edee.

"Hey," said Lucie, sort of meeting her eyes, while letting herself be swept towards the counter.

Edee and Scotty followed.

"Lucie," said Cass. "Ty."

"Hi," said Lucie, smiling. "I feel like I already know you."

"I know what you mean." Ty leaned on the counter. "We loved the videos you made. How is it being back?"

"Different," said Lucie.

"It's so amazing to see you," said Cass. She squealed. "I can't believe you're actually here. And it's so much better it was a surprise."

"What was it for?" said Maddie. Her eyes strayed towards Edee.

Lucie moved towards one of the stools and climbed up. "Mum wanted to. It doesn't matter."

Scotty nudged Edee.

"I hope she wants to come back every month," said Cass. "It's like we haven't seen you for years."

"Loads has changed," said Lucie.

"Do you know Scotty?" said Cass.

Lucie shook her head. "We met yesterday."

"We don't know him either," said Cass. "Edee's been hiding him."

"No I haven't," said Edee.

"Here I am." Scotty waved.

"Luce, we were thinking of a film night tonight," said Cass. "At mine. You're not flying until tomorrow, right?"

"Yeah," said Lucie.

"This is the best day ever," said Cass. She climbed onto

219

the stool next to Lucie's. "Tell us about every single thing you've seen since you left."

"You already know most of it," said Lucie.

"I don't care," said Cass. "I want to hear it again."

"Hang on, I need to look busy," said Ty. He drummed his fingers on the counter. "What drinks?"

"Whatever takes the longest to make," said Cass. "When's your break?"

"Not for half an hour." Ty opened the fridge door and took out several cartons of milk.

Maybe Kitty would come and cover for him then.

"Come on." Cass nudged Lucie's leg. "Tell us the best thing that's happened in the last two months."

Scotty leaned forward and whispered by Edee's ear, "Lines?"

She nodded. All six of them sitting there, looking out through the lines they'd made up. And the other people in the cafe too. And everyone else. Humans being inside lines that shimmered and changed and sometimes dropped away. It was so, so interesting. It was beautiful when you knew. It was hard to think it had ever seemed anything but fascinating and beautiful.

"It's got to be the people," said Lucie. "There are so many incredible people. Sometimes you meet someone, spend a day or two with them, and it's like you know everything about them." Her eyes strayed to Edee's.

Edee smiled.

Lucie looked away. She crossed her arms. "And the food. And the new stuff every single day."

"You're so lucky," said Cass. "Would your parents adopt me? Is the van big enough for an extra person?"

"Two," said Ty.

Cass grinned.

"Come and visit," said Lucie. "Christmas or Easter or something."

"I wish," said Cass. "Make sure you tell my mum how great it is tonight. I'm going to have to work on her." She looked all around. "Is Freddie here? I want to ask him about a job again."

Ty shook his head. "It's his day off. I'll remind him again tomorrow."

"Is Kitty here?" said Edee.

"Who?" said Cass.

"Kitty," said Edee. "She works here waitressing. Sometimes cleaning."

"Kitty?" Ty's mouth turned down at the edges like it was a peculiar question.

"She was here when we came before," said Edee. "The first time. Cleaning." She glanced to Cass. "She was in the bathroom when you came and got me."

Cass shook her head. "I don't remember."

"Kitty," said Edee again.

"Nope," said Ty. "Negative. Nada. No Kitties in the cafe." He laughed. Cass did too.

But he did know her because Kitty had known about Cass. "Are you sure?"

"Yes," said Ty. "Positive. There's a photo of everyone over there if you don't believe me."

There was a challenge in his tone, but she slid from the stool anyway and headed towards the noticeboard. The photo showed fifteen or so people. Kitty was not one of them. She scanned the picture again. No, wait, there she was. Something inside her soared, but the next time she blinked the face had gone. She blinked again. Still gone. "When was this taken?"

Ty poured some milk into a jug and held it under the frother. He raised his voice. "About a week ago. Freddie got mug shots of us to go on the website. They took that at the end."

"It's everyone?" said Edee.

"Yep," said Ty. "Want me to name them?"

Lucie, Cass, and Maddie were all watching her. "I must've been mistaken." She sat back down.

"Another Jonathan?" muttered Scotty.

"Maybe," murmured Edee. How utterly, utterly curious.

"Edes?" said Maddie. "Are you okay?"

"Yeah," said Edee. It was true. She was okay, she knew she was. So were the others. So was Kitty, whoever, wherever, whatever she was. Edee glanced up and smiled. The room around her seemed so very different. There were no lines. None. Of course, she thought. *Of course.*

THE END

As you think, so you shall hear.

— SYDNEY BANKS

ACKNOWLEDGMENTS

First of all, I would like to thank my family and friends, who mostly did not know I was writing, but who provided excellent, much needed, reasons to step away from the computer. Special thanks go to L and J, my fantastic niece and nephew, who taught me so much about life before the lines.

Huge thanks go to Kate Angelella for her brilliant editing, Anna Woodbine for her awesome cover design, Kate Habberley for coming to the proofreading rescue, and Stephanie Drake for being so patient with (seemingly) endless tweaks to the manuscript long after it should have been finished. I need to hurry up and write a new manuscript so I get to work with you all again.

The idea for *The Edee Story* popped into my head when I was listening to Dicken Bettinger give a talk at the Three Principles UK Conference in 2016. It was my first Three Principles conference and it's fascinating to look back at how things have unfolded since—life has such an interesting way of working out. My thanks go to everyone involved in putting on the UK conference.

While my first published book, *Art Beholding*, was written

while I was on a practitioner course with One Thought, this one was rewritten while I had returned for the listening programme. Thank you to everyone involved in the 2019/20 course for providing the backdrop to this period of writing. Particular thanks go to the Saturday morning 'Fresh Look At' crew. Starting the weekend with you guys is always a treat.

Finally, thank you to you for reading *The Edee Story*. I have learned so much by putting my work out into the world. If you are someone who longs to create but keeps feeling fearful, or if you're curious about the Three Principles in general, there is a resources page on my website: claremerrett.com

ALSO BY CLARE MERRETT

Art Beholding

Printed in Great Britain
by Amazon